RIVER WOODS

Renaissance
Valley Publishing

Woods, River

Contents

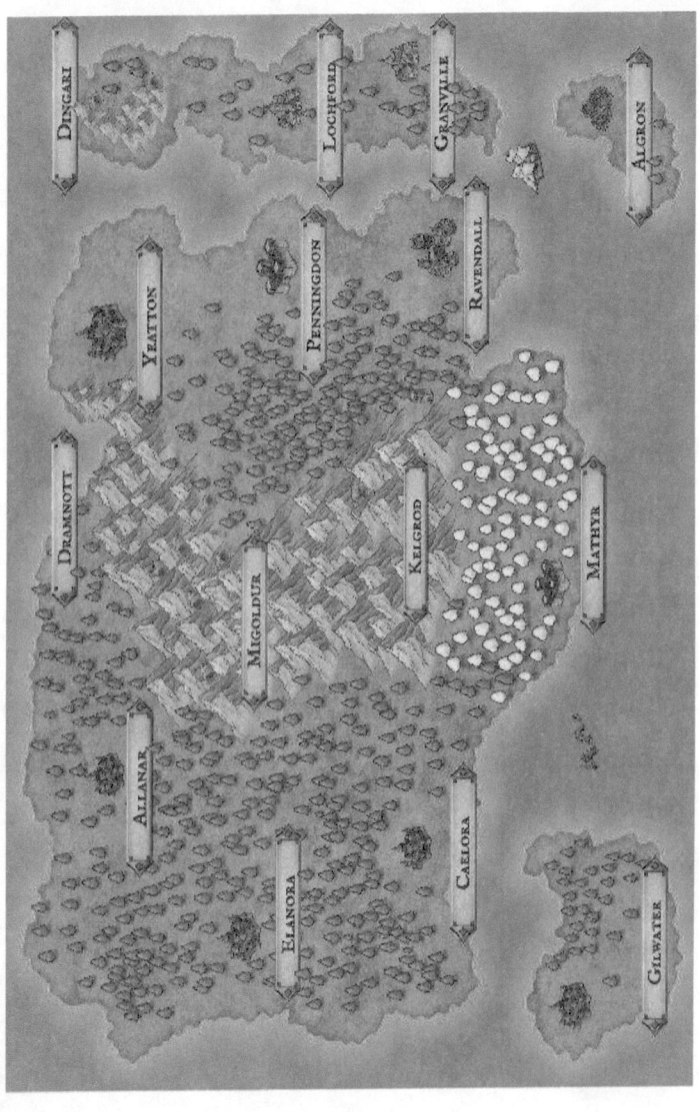

Assassinating Beauty

Chapter 1

What is death? Is it the absence of life? Or is life the absence of death? Life is movement, action. Death is stillness. The ultimate cessation of the body. Not always peace for the soul of the one who passed, but silence and serenity for the strangers left behind. Thallan liked silence and serenity. In a kingdom that was nothing but chaos and noise, he sought the quiet and stillness that so often eludes us. He was the bringer of death.

From his position on the rooftop, Thallan gazed out over the city past slanted eaves and twisted spires to the glittering expanse of the sea beyond. Even from that distance, he could see the motion of the waves. The rhythmic churning of the water morphed into a more riotous commotion as the dock flowed into the streets. They were littered with humans pouring out of the theater, talking, laughing, living too much.

He raised his gaze to the stars. Even his elven eyes couldn't discern their motion. Their constancy grounded him. If only he could close his ears to the harsh tones of the human voices and his nose to their vile smells, he might be able to find some peace in this strange land.

1

A light breeze blew over his face, and Thallan reached up to readjust his black hood. The motion was the first discernable one he had made since he took up this post an hour ago. He knew how to be still. His cloak blended into the dark tiles of the roof and the shadows of the night. He knew how to be invisible.

The elf frowned as he turned his attention back to the guards patrolling inside the high manor walls. He had a job to do before he could return to the sanctuary of his new home. He leaped from the roof onto the wall, then glided quietly to the ground. Melting into the shadows, he kept a watchful eye on the sentries.

Four of them stood guard in the front, with four more in the back. Two watched each side. One walked the perimeter in a clockwise direction, and another walked counterclockwise. It would take one minute after the commotion began for the guards in the back to arrive. The one patrolling clockwise would require the same amount of time. The four on the sides and the one patrolling counterclockwise would arrive in a matter of seconds. No problem. They were only humans, after all.

Thallan pulled off his face covering before stepping into the light. Warriors had a right to see the face of their enemy. For a split second, the guards only stared at him, stunned, as if he were a ghost suddenly appearing in their midst. But he was not the one who would be haunting this place.

When their minds caught up to the reality of what they saw, the air filled with the roar of voices and the clang of armor. Almost instantly, they had him surrounded. He let them. They were warriors, after all. Even if they were human, no warrior deserved to die feeling like a complete failure.

"State your business," one of the men demanded.

"I'm here to assassinate your master," Thallan replied casually.

"You can't be serious."

Thallan's face remained emotionless, and his voice cold. "I don't joke."

"Enough!" the man thundered. "Kill him!"

Thallan raised his hands, blades suddenly filling them. One of the men dashed forward, sword held high. He didn't get far. Blood spewed from his mouth, and he fell to his knees, clutching his chest. He stared in bewilderment at Thallan's now motionless hand. The steel in the elf's grasp dripped with blood, whereas only an instant ago, it had been clean. He had heard rumors of the impossible speed the elves could command but never believed it. His body slumped lifelessly to the ground.

Instantly, panic filled the courtyard, and gasps of terror rose from every human throat. The other sentries scrambled away from him. An expression of resigned patience spread across Thallan's face as if he were waiting for a dog to attack, knowing he would have to put it down when it did.

"I have no quarrel with you. I only want your master. Stand aside and let me pass."

Regaining his courage, the guard captain stepped forward. "Take him down, or Lord Byron will have your heads!" he shouted. "He can't kill us all!"

Doubt filled a few of their faces, and some hesitated, but Thallan gave them no more time to decide. The next wave would arrive soon. He sprang into action.

The moonlight reflected off his blades as they streaked through the air, leaving trails of silver in their wake. Droplets and ribbons of red flew in every direction. The grass changed from a beautiful, lush green to a deep crimson as blood poured from his victims. The guard captain was the only one granted time for any audible reaction, and his horrified scream cut off abruptly as Thallan's blade cleanly severed his throat.

Thallan waited as that last body fell—waited to feel something, anything. A moment of welcomed peace and silence was all that he found. Even that didn't give him the satisfaction he had expected. The magic wouldn't allow him any emotion while he was in the midst of the curse's control. But a moment was all he could take. He still had a job to do.

He turned and entered the house. A female servant looked up from dusting the banister and stared in horror at the blood-soaked specter intruding on her domain. A piercing scream ripped from her throat. She stood, frozen in fear, as he slowly approached. He tilted his head to the side, examining her curiously. Her wide eyes didn't move. Her body appeared stiff in its almost complete motionlessness. Only her chest heaved with her rapid breaths. If not for her upright stance and unsteady breathing, she could pass as one of the deceased.

He leaned in closer. She leaned back. Her dusting cloth fell from her hand and floated to

4

the floor. Her breaths grew quicker and harsher. Was it possible for someone to die of fright? He was tempted to see. She seemed so close. But his experiment was not to be.

Six guards swarmed down the stairs. Thallan stepped away from the girl and raised his blades. Awoken by the approaching men, the girl regained her senses and turned and ran.

He said nothing to his victims this time, yet he was just as relentless in his movements. They collapsed all around him like marionettes with severed strings.

He made his way up the grand marble staircase and through the elaborately decorated halls, his boots leaving gruesome stains on the lush carpeting. He encountered no more resistance until he approached the master's chamber. Two men stood guard outside. Their broad chests and wide stances spoke of a confidence rather bold considering the fate of their comrades. Thallan paused. He would allow them to make the first move. Their courage warranted that.

The man on the right began to advance, but instead of approaching the assassin, he tried to ease around behind him. So, they weren't fools. That would not save them, but it did make their inevitable demise more tragic. Thallan recognized the fact even though he could feel no remorse for it.

Once the man was in position, they both attacked simultaneously. The elf responded more slowly than he had before. Their movements were more controlled. Their motions faster. Their strikes more calculated. If there had been five or six of them and he weren't on a job, he might enjoy sparring with them. As it was, he did not have time to play. After allowing them sufficient time to feel they had done well, he quickly dispatched them and entered the chamber.

"Please spare me. My master is not here. Please, I beg you."

Thallan stared down at the small, pathetic, quivering man kneeling before him. He closed his eyes and tried to feel pity, empathy, anything, but nothing came. Only a dull, steady urge to kill. A drive that he couldn't ignore.

With a burst of bravery, or perhaps fear, the servant took this opportunity to remove a small dagger hidden in his worn-out boot. He stuck it with as much force as he could muster into Thallan's thigh. The assassin's eyes snapped open, and he glared at the little man.

The servant gasped at the ice in the elf's steely blue eyes. He released the dagger and frantically backed away, realizing that was the last decision he would ever make. He barely had time to regret it before a strong hand grasped his neck, and he was lifted off his feet.

With a flick of Thallan's wrist, the servant went limp. The elf opened his hand and watched the body fall to the floor with a thud. A slow handclap sounded from the doorway of an adjacent room. Thallan's eyes narrowed as he turned to the richly dressed man standing there.

"That was not very smart of my servant, but he was never overly bright." The man stepped out of the doorway and ambled toward Thallan. "You are cold, efficient, and a merciless killer. What would it take to have you work for me?"

Thallan's face remained impassive as he bent to pick up the sword he had dropped. "Lord Byron, I presume." He slid both blades into the scabbards on his back and crossed his arms over his chest.

The man smiled and nodded. Thallan studied him. He had just watched his servant murdered, yet he showed no anger, no fear. Thallan, too, had felt nothing, but that was a different matter altogether.

"You are not outraged at the death of your servant, of all the guards I slaughtered?" he asked curiously.

Lord Byron shrugged. "People can be replaced. It's an inconvenience for sure, but that is all. Someone like you, however, is special. You would be a great prize for me to add to my staff. If you work for me, I will pay whatever you ask. And you may kill whomever you wish," he added, running his eyes over Thallan's blood-soaked clothes.

Lord Byron suddenly found himself hovering a few feet off the ground. What felt like a band of iron cut off his breath. His hands darted to his neck and gripped the elf's fingers, vainly trying to pull them away. His eyes widened in confusion. What was happening? Was this man going to kill him? He couldn't kill *him*. He was rich. He had offered him a job. No one refused him. He was Lord Byron!

The lord's attempt to speak was thwarted by a lack of oxygen and the constriction of his throat. Thallan raised a finger on his free hand, silencing him.

"No need for meaningless words, human. I know what you wish to ask. What my targets always want to ask—who it is that is granting their bodies the stillness of death. I will satisfy your curiosity."

As Lord Byron felt his life fade away, the last thing he heard was a whisper. "I am the Beast."

"What's the point of it all?" Isa thought as she wrapped a bandage around the man's bleeding arm. She recognized him. He had been there for a concussion only two weeks ago.

He cried out in pain as she pulled the bandage tight before tying it. She had little sympathy for him. Likely, he would be back before the month was out. Sometimes, she wondered why she bothered.

The majority of the people who came to the poor hospital were reprobates or bandits, usually sent there by other reprobates or bandits. She leaned back on her heels, her hands resting in her lap, as she gazed around the room. It was probably the cleanest place in the whole Downs, which wasn't saying much.

She stood and untied her apron, dropping it in the laundry basket by the door.

"That was the last one."

Dr. Monroe looked up from the pile of papers on his desk and gave her a tired smile. His eyes drooped a little, and a scattering of gray scruff dotted his chin like frost on a window. He had been there all night and half the day before. But even though all the patients were resting peacefully, and they were unlikely to get any more that night, Isa knew he would stay awake until the day shift arrived. Part of her wished she could stay with him and let him rest, but the other part was glad she had to get back before anyone missed her. Her bed beckoned.

"Thanks for staying so late to help with the victims of the bar fight. I know you must be tired."

"It was no problem. I'm glad I was still here to help. I know you're tired as well. Have a good night."

"Have a good night, dear." He glanced out past her form standing in the open doorway, and a frown wrinkled his forehead. "It's quite late. Do you want me to walk you home?"

Isa just laughed. "I think what you mean to say is that it's quite early. Most people have retired to their beds by now, even cutthroats and thieves."

"Perhaps, but still be careful. You never know for sure who lurks in the darkness."

"I will." She pulled her hood as far over her face as it would go. The people in that part of town knew her and the work she did in the hospital. She had patched most of them up at one time or another after all. That afforded her some protection since they had a begrudging respect for her, but it wasn't a respect she was willing to bet her life on.

Isa stayed close to the buildings instead of walking down the middle of the street, and she wrapped her fingers tightly around the dagger strapped to her waist. It was that strange time between night and day when early risers hadn't yet awakened and those who preferred the darker hours had finally retired. Isa struggled to keep her eyes open and her feet moving as weariness threatened to overtake her. She shivered in the chilly air and pulled her cloak more snuggly about her body, thankful for the long woolen stockings she had decided to wear.

Gradually, she began to notice the loud silence that filled the night. So loud she imagined she could hear it. It was as if the world held its breath, waiting for something. She moved as quietly as she could, fearful of making a sound. Wide awake now, her eyes darted from shadow to shadow. Why was it so quiet? She had never been out at this time of day before. It felt unnatural, otherworldly. Was that normal?

She nearly jumped out of her skin when a dog barked in the distance. For a moment, it eased the tension that had gripped her insides. She wasn't all alone after all. But only for a moment. Now, her imagination formed creatures and beasts in the shadows around her—or even worse, men.

One particular shadow grabbed her attention. Had it just moved? It appeared to shift before her very eyes, a deeper, darker shade, flowing along the side of a building.

She gasped, the sound hitting her ears like thunder. The darkness paused, and she held her breath, her eyes glued to the sight. Slowly, it began moving again. This time in her direction. Her mind raced. Her instincts screamed at her to flee. But that small part of her, surrounded and shielded by a sense of indestructibility, was curious.

The shadow expanded as if the building were growing a new appendage right before her eyes. As it shifted away from the wall, it began to morph into a recognizable form. A man. A tall man in a dark cloak. This was no mystery, no fantasy. This was a real, familiar danger. Isa started to run when the man stumbled slightly and fell against the wall.

At first, she assumed he was drunk. That would be the most likely scenario and not unheard of in this part of town, even at that time of night. She intended to leave him to his own devices, but she hesitated. Something was off. A drunk man in that condition should have thrown up or passed out by now. He would at least have moved on. This man remained where he was as if he had suddenly turned to stone.

Slowly, she approached him. Her instincts once again screamed to be heard, and once again, she ignored them. She did, however, allow the fear to flow through her muscles, pulling them tight. It would give her speed if she needed it.

Perhaps it was the darkness, or perhaps it was the silent, empty street, but there was something about the figure, even from this distance, that seemed dangerous. Deadly. But she was a nurse, and the man was obviously experiencing some problem.

Her heart beat so strongly, she imagined she could hear it. She could definitely feel it. She spoke up in a quiet voice as she grew closer to him, still hesitant to break the silence.

"Are you alright?"

She saw only darkness under the shadow of his hood. Her body instinctively leaned away. Was he even a man? The being turned its head to face her, and she caught a glimpse of two eyes. She half expected them to be lit with red flames, but they appeared human enough, though she couldn't see their color in the dim light. So, it was a man after all. She examined the darkness beneath them, attempting, but failing, to determine his features.

"It's okay. I'm a nurse. I can help. Are you injured?"

The man simply stared at her. The silence grew uncomfortable, and Isa considered leaving. Even if he was hurt, she wouldn't force her help on him. Just as she started to go, a deep voice came from the midst of the hood.

"Yes."

For a moment, she forgot what she had asked and just stared at him blankly.

"Yes, I am injured," he clarified.

"Oh," she said, moving closer. "Where are you hurt?"

The man swept his cloak to the side, and she saw the dagger sticking out of his thigh. She couldn't tell how much the injury had bled because his pants were covered in dark stains. Was it all blood? If so, a great deal of it was obviously not from his wound. She gasped in horror as her eyes traveled up to his face. His whole body was covered with the dark stains.

Who was this man? More importantly, what had he done? She took a deep breath and squared her shoulders. Regardless, she needed to get him to the hospital, and quickly.

"Can you walk if you lean on me?"

He moved away from the wall and slung his arm over her shoulder; though he was so much taller than she was, she wasn't sure how much she'd be able to assist him. She couldn't help but think about how her cloak would be stained beyond redemption as she wrapped her arm around his waist. Maybe she could die it a deep red.

They made their way awkwardly down the street, the weight on her shoulder growing steadily as the man slumped lower. She glanced over at him. His eyes were closed under the black hood, and faint lines had formed beside them in what Isa could only assume was a grimace of pain.

He stumbled again, and his hood slid from his head. Light hair crowned his head, disappearing into the dark cloth he had tied around the lower part of his face. She almost dropped him when she saw pointed ears protruding from the top of the fabric.

"You're an elf!"

"I am."

She took a sharp breath, frozen with indecision.

"Does that mean you will no longer help me?"

She couldn't take her eyes off his ears, but his words finally penetrated the fog of her surprise. She stared down at the ground as she considered. *Did* that mean she wouldn't help him? She didn't want to.

Nursing thieves and cutthroats was bad enough, but at least they were human. She despised elves. Was that blood on his clothes? Had he killed someone that night? She wondered who. She squeezed her eyes shut against the flood of emotions that suddenly raged through her as visions from her past seeped into her mind. She ruthlessly shoved the images away. She couldn't think about those things now. Not with him here, so close. So dangerous.

The feeling of his muscular arm wrapped around her shoulders emphasized his strength and her current vulnerability, but it also reminded her of his injury.

When she became a nurse, she had made a vow to help those in need. However, she was only a part-time volunteer nurse. Surely, that meant she didn't have to be on duty at all times, didn't it?

Guilt battled with anger. Duty with disdain. The conflict raged for several moments. The elf waited quietly, but the pressure of his weight steadily increased. Isa gritted her teeth and shifted his arm on her shoulder. She would tend to his wound. Then, she would decide what to do with him.

"I'll help you, but I don't think it would be wise for us to go to the hospital. There are many men there who would love nothing more than to get their hands on an injured elf." Her eyes again raked his stained clothes. "Though it doesn't appear that would be much of a problem for you, I'd imagine you would like to be able to rest at some point."

"Take me where you will. I am at your disposal."

The pressure on her shoulders continued to grow as they made their way down the street, and his feet stumbled more often on the uneven cobblestones. He had slumped over so much that his face was now even with hers. She wrapped her other arm around his stomach to help hold him up. She would need to find someplace for him soon.

Up ahead, she spotted a cottage belonging to another nurse from the hospital, and she headed toward it. Struggling under the increasing weight, she banged on the door frantically. She wouldn't be able to hold him much longer. Her arm felt like it was about to fall off. She shook him lightly.

"Don't pass out on me yet. You're too heavy for me to lift on my own. If you fall here, you'll stay here."

The threat seemed to do the trick. Her burden lightened slightly, but she banged on the door again. It opened a crack, and her friend's face peaked out.

"Carrie. Let us in. I'm about to drop him."

"What in the world?" The girl pulled the door open and rushed to the man's other side.

"Watch out for the dagger in his leg."

"Dagger?"

Carrie glanced down at the protruding handle.

"Oh, my goodness."

She pulled his other arm over her shoulder and helped carefully maneuver him inside.

"I'll replace your sheets," Isa promised as they lowered the large, blood-soaked man down onto the tiny bed. His limp form offered no resistance.

"Who is this, and why are you bringing him here? We do have a hospital in this town, you know."

Isa straightened up and rubbed her aching back.

"I couldn't take him to the hospital."

"Why not?"

"He's an elf," she said as she began rummaging around in her friend's cabinet for supplies.

Carrie gazed down at him curiously. "Is he really?"

"Look at his ears."

The girl's face filled with awe as her eyes traced the lines of the unfamiliar shapes.

"I've never seen an elf before." Her eyes moved to his face covering. "I wonder what he looks like. I've heard that elves are quite handsome."

"Ugh. He's an elf, Carrie."

The girl shrugged. "He's still a man."

"I don't want to hear it. In fact, I *want* to *not* hear it. Or see it. Do me a favor, will you."

"What?"

"Don't remove that cloth."

"What? Why?" Carrie's hand froze in midair, only inches away from the covering.

Isa poured some salt into a glass of water and mixed it thoroughly.

"He's an elf. I hate elves. I don't want to be distracted from that by a pretty face."

Carrie snorted. "Are your emotions so easily influenced?"

Isa shrugged. "Aren't everyone's? If there's one thing I've learned in life, it's that beauty can blind people to many faults. I don't want to fall into that trap."

"Very well. He can keep this secret."

Carrie lifted his legs and slung them up on the bed. His feet hung over the edge, making it much easier to remove his tall boots, though it probably wouldn't be very comfortable for him.

Isa washed her hands and brought the supplies over, setting them on a chair. Kneeling

16

beside the bed, she took a pair of scissors and cut his pants leg away from the wound.

"Are you ready?"

Carrie picked up a couple of cloths and nodded. Isa grabbed the handle of the blade and carefully pulled it out. Carrie immediately covered the wound with the cloths and applied pressure. The girls watched and waited. The fabric quickly took on a dark red hue, blood saturating the cloth. Isa positioned another bundle and quickly moved it into place when Carrie took hers away.

They had to change the cloths two more times before the bleeding stopped and Isa could wash out the wound. By then, the new day had dawned, and Carrie had to get to the hospital.

"I'm sure I don't have to remind you not to tell anyone about this."

Carrie snorted. "About what? The elf, who is covered in blood, lying in my bed? No. You don't have to remind me."

Isa laughed. "Good."

She sighed as her fellow nurse left the cottage. She was almost finished. Only a little longer, and she could rest. She threaded a needle and jabbed it into his leg. Now that the immediate danger to him was over, her anger resurfaced. She stitched the wound closed, making no attempt to be gentle. It seemed almost an insult that he wasn't awake to appreciate the pain she was trying to inflict on him.

Standing at the table, washing the blood from her hands, Isa stared into the distance, planning. How could she get the city guard here without talking to them directly? She didn't want anyone to know she was there. She was a lady of the court, after all. If her peers ever discovered she had spent the night in the Downs, taking care of an elf, nonetheless, she would be ostracized. Her reputation would never recover. It would be bad enough if they found out she worked in the hospital here, but an elf...

She could send one of the street children with a message, but the threat still remained. An elf was big news. Word would get out, and everyone would want to know who was with him. Her face was easily described and widely recognizable. Besides, the elf was in Carrie's house. She didn't want to get her friend in trouble.

Isa groaned. A wave of exhaustion washed over her. She couldn't think. She needed to rest first. She'd take a quick nap and then figure something out. She practically fell into the chair by the bed, her eyes closing of their own accord. Within seconds, she was out.

The air smelled different, not as vile as usual—clean with an undertone of herbs. Thallan dug deeply into his mind, trying to remember what had happened—where he was. Like a figure approaching through a fog, his memories began to take form.

He had carelessly allowed himself to get stabbed. There was a girl, and she had taken him to a house. After that was only darkness.

The sound of slow, steady breathing brought his attention to his surroundings. Someone slept. He opened his eyes and glanced around the small room. Neatly but scarcely furnished, it was devoid of life except for him and the girl asleep in a tall, wing-back chair beside the bed.

Her rich brown hair lay spread around her in waves, framing soft, rounded cheeks, a small nose, and rosy lips. Her beauty rivaled that of the elves, but that fact was only noted and set aside. Thallan was accustomed to beauty. He had been surrounded by it his entire life. It didn't affect him.

He silently swung his legs off the bed and winced at the dull throb in his thigh. He could feel that the wound had already begun healing. How long had he been there?

Thallan glanced down at the neat row of stitches standing in dark contrast to his paler skin. The foolish girl. Didn't she know that was unnecessary—that elves were capable of accelerated healing? Of course, she didn't. She was only a human, after all. Humans knew nothing.

He located his boots and pulled them on, then stood, gradually testing his weight on his injured leg. It was still too weak. He would need to give it more time to heal before making the long trek home, and he had another job to do tonight. He might as well stay in town. He needed to find a place where he could hide out until nightfall. His eyes moved back to the sleeping girl.

Could he wait here? That would be the most convenient, but that idea didn't satisfy him. She would wake soon and undoubtedly protest when he insisted she remain inside. He would have to forcefully restrain her. Even if she was only a human, she had assisted him in a time of need and had shown great courage in doing so. He couldn't in good conscience reward her so harshly.

Why *had* she helped him? He peered down at her, examining her sleeping visage, trying to deduce her motives through the gentle inhale and exhale of her breath. She hated elves. His memory readily supplied that bit of information. Her tone, her demeanor, and the half step she had taken away from him when she saw his ears left no doubt about that.

So, why? Was it possible that a human had the potential for kindness simply for the sake of kindness? He didn't believe it. But as he could offer no other explanation, he would save the thought for further contemplation at a later date. Now, he needed to find someplace to hide. Though he hadn't made the conscious decision, he knew he wouldn't stay there.

Thallan stood beside the window and moved the curtain aside a few inches. Cautiously peering out, he studied the street and the buildings running alongside it. There, a few blocks down. The building had been almost entirely consumed by fire, yet a portion remained that appeared sufficient to meet his needs. Now, he just had to reach it without drawing undue attention to himself.

While the street wasn't empty, neither was it crowded. Only a few people ambled by, and they appeared to be intentionally minding their own business. Thallan watched them. No one looked around. No one spoke. Everyone kept their eyes on the ground and their attention on their path.

Thallan glanced back at the girl. Her clothing was plain, but the material was clearly good quality. What was she doing in a place like this? Poverty seeped out of every crevice, even in this cottage. Some of the furniture was rather nice, for a poverty-stricken area, but it was old and worn and there was very little of it. The girl didn't belong here.

He shook his head in bewilderment and turned back to the window. The cowering atmosphere of the neighborhood would work in his favor. It would be unlikely anyone would take note of him. They would undoubtedly try hard not to, but if they did, he knew how to be frightening. He could make them look away.

He pulled his hood up over his head and adjusted his face covering. With one last glance at the sleeping girl, he slipped out of the cottage and made his way to his temporary shelter.

The ballroom was alive with light and color. Glass chandeliers sparkled from the glow of a multitude of candles, casting tiny rainbows around the room. Diamonds, rubies, emeralds, and a plethora of other gemstones glittered from the necks, ears, wrists, and hands of countless bodies. The music, loud and cheerful, bounced off the walls, and dancers whirled across the floor, the ladies' bright dresses a flurry of movement.

Most of the chatter resonating through the space centered around one specific couple. All eyes followed them, some hungrily, others jealously, but few kindly. The Penningdon court was not known for its kindness.

The couple, who was the focus of all this interest, twirled to the music, oblivious to the

21

attention they were receiving. Lady Isabella Kantrell's green silk gown swirled as Lord Alistair Tremain spun her in a graceful circle. She laughed in delight.

She felt almost giddy. She loved dancing, but tonight, even more so than usual. After the fright and stress of meeting the elf the previous night and the frustration at his escape, she needed this release. She had accepted that it hadn't turned out as she wished. But she had also accepted that there was nothing more she could do about it. So, she decided to put the incident from her mind and think about it no longer. Now, she focused on the moment and let all her negative emotions flow out of her as she twirled and whirled around the room.

"You are so beautiful," Lord Alistair commented, drawn in by her musical laughter.

She smiled and placed a hand over her heart playfully. "Why, thank you, kind sir."

Lord Alistair pulled her closer as the music slowed, and she adapted her pace to his. One of his hands pressed into her lower back, and the other gently but firmly squeezed hers.

"Marry me," he said.

Isa pretended she hadn't heard him. "I still have several gentlemen waiting to dance with me," she said, subtly pulling away from him.

His grip on her waist tightened. "Isa."

She winced. He was using her nickname. She didn't like this assumption of a familiarity she didn't share. "Such informality, Lord Alistair. I'm not sure that's entirely proper," she said teasingly.

"Answer me!" he demanded under his breath.

Isa looked away and mumbled, "I can't."

Alistair sighed and released her, running his hand through his pure black hair. Isa twisted uncomfortably as she now noticed that more than a few curious eyes were on them.

"What can I do to change your mind?" Lord Alistair spoke, turning Isa's attention back to him.

She put on the best sad face she could muster and said quietly, "I'm sorry, my lord." She curtsied to him and walked away.

"Just look at her go, the little witch." Princess Nixa scowled as she watched Isa's hasty retreat from the side of the ballroom.

"I'm sure she just broke yet another heart," she said with a sad pout that could almost have passed for real emotion if it hadn't immediately morphed into a sneer. "The arrogant little thing thinks nobody is good enough for her."

The group of ladies huddled around her nodded in agreement as Nixa smirked. "Why don't we see what she has to say?"

Her entourage giggled and followed as the princess stalked after Isa. They found her alone on the balcony, staring at the night sky. Lord William McDowel was walking away from her, having been dismissed just as Lord Alistair had.

"Lady Isabella." The princess's voice dripped with derision. She raised her chin, causing the diamonds and rubies in her tiara to twinkle.

Isa sighed. Her giddiness had evaporated with Lord Alistair's proposal, and her frustration had returned with that of Lord Williams. Superficial. All of them. She received proposals almost daily, but none of the men knew anything about her. Only that she was beautiful. She'd rather never marry at all than marry someone who only wanted her for her looks.

Now, the princess and her cronies were there. Of course, they wouldn't let her have a moment's peace.

"Princess Nixa," Isa said with a slight curtsey.

The princess scowled. "I don't know why you even bother with the formalities. We both know you haven't any respect for me."

Isa chuckled. "That much is true. It's your title that I curtsey to, not you."

Nixa's face flushed brightly, from her neck to her obsidian tresses. Fire blazed in her gaze.

"You have broken another heart, I see," she said, pretending that she cared about the feelings of the men she toyed with regularly herself. "This time, it is a heart I wish to have in my possession."

Isabella shrugged. "I'm sorry?"

A servant appeared at that moment and whispered into the princess's ear, and a smile spread across her face.

"It would appear Lord Alistair wishes to have a dance with me after all," she said, shooting Isa a triumphant look.

Isa curtsied again and turned to continue staring at the stars, effectively dismissing the irritating royal.

Princess Nixa glared at her before marching back into the ballroom with her followers trailing closely behind.

"It is a pleasure to dance with you, Lord Alistair," Princess Nixa said as she curtsied elegantly before the tall noble. She beamed at him, the diamonds sparkling in her black updo matching the twinkle in her eyes.

Lord Alistair gave her a tight grin in return. "The pleasure is all mine, Your Highness."

His eyes searched the ballroom for Isa as they danced. The princess in his arms was stunning. There was no denying that. Princess Nixa possessed a dark, daring beauty with her black hair, pale skin, and bright red lips. But he didn't want a dark, daring wife. He wanted someone more malleable, someone softer, sweeter. With her chocolate brown hair and deep green eyes, Isa's beauty was soft and sweet. Anyone who looked like that would be the perfect woman for him.

He sighed, trying to stay focused on the girl he was with. Regrettably, his duty as a noble required him to dance with the princess at these events. He would rather be with Isa, but one did not offend the royal family lightly.

"… don't know why men like her so much. She always breaks their hearts and has no problem flirting with everyone. You know, she's been that way since we were kids, always batting her eyelashes at young boys, causing them to fall helplessly in love with her." The princess's voice brought him back to the moment.

Alistair frowned. "Of whom are you speaking?"

Princess Nixa scoffed. "Lady Isabella, of course. Haven't you been listening to a word I've said?"

Lord Alistair almost laughed out loud but managed to contain it. Sweet Isabella a flirt?

Never. Someone with Nixa's coloring, maybe, but not Isabella.

"As I was saying," Princess Nixa continued, "she's honestly the worst lady at court. If her father hadn't been my father's prime minister, I would have never had the displeasure of knowing her."

Lord Alistair's expression darkened, and he stepped back from the princess. Nixa stopped talking at this unexpected move in the middle of the dance floor. She glanced uncomfortably at the couples swirling around them, then back to her reluctant partner.

"I had the honor of dancing with Lady Isabella only a short while ago and heard no malicious words from her. I have been with you barely five minutes, Your Highness, and all I've heard you speak about is the supposed ill manner of the other lady. Forgive me if I find it distasteful and beg to take leave of this dance."

He turned around without waiting for a reply and walked away. Once again, a blush of crimson crept onto Princess Nixa's cheeks as the eyes of the room focused on her. Humiliation welled up inside her, quickly replaced by a burning anger.

Everyone thought Isabella was so kind and gentle and perfect. She may have all the most eligible bachelors chasing after her now, but Nixa was still considered quite beautiful herself, and she was a princess. Being a princess gave her a power the daughter of a former prime minister could never have.

Fueled by her indignation, Nixa stormed out of the ballroom and headed towards the balcony with her ladies-in-waiting, again, trailing behind her like faithful puppies.

Isa still stood there, though she had moved over to the corner where she was more hidden from those inside. Good. The privacy suited Nixa just fine. Isa turned around just as the princess reached her. The poor girl had no time to react before a resounding slap landed on her left cheek.

The metallic taste of blood almost overwhelmed her self-control. She bit down hard on her tongue to contain her mounting rage—to override the temptation of unleashing that rage on Nixa. Her gloved hands formed into tight fists as she glared at the princess.

When she spoke, however, her voice remained calm. "I'm sure you have a good reason for choosing to act in so unbecoming a way."

Princess Nixa snorted. "Stay away from Alistair," she growled.

Isabella paused, then suddenly laughed.

"*You* are jealous of *me*," she said incredulously. "You. You have most of the men in the kingdom chasing you."

"Not the best ones," Nixa said with a snarl. "Somehow, you seem able to mesmerize them. I can't imagine why." She waved her hand up and down, indicating Isa's body. "You're such a skinny, faded thing."

Isa's anger flared, but she kept it under control. "Perhaps they don't like your temper. Or maybe it's your pride or ego that puts them off. Maybe you should check that before you go making ridiculous demands of other people."

With those words, Isa shoved past the ladies and returned to the ballroom.

Nixa's gaze burned as she fixed her sapphire blue eyes on Isa's back. The very air seemed to crackle with her rage. That was it. Isabella had insulted her for the last time. Princess Nixa was determined to ensure she would never stand in her way again, no matter what it took.

Chapter 2

Thallan studied the letter he'd just retrieved from his contact in town. His new target was to be a lady. He frowned and stared into the fire. He didn't like killing women. He had, in the past. Goblin women often fought beside their men on the battlefield. However, he had never killed a female off the battlefield before.

The target was a human, however, and humans were the enemy. If not for the actions of the human king of Yeatton, the goblins and the elves would never have gone to war. So many of his people would never have died, and he would never have been cursed. True, this was the Kingdom of Penningdon, not Yeatton, but humans were humans no matter where they lived.

He glanced back down at the letter, going over the middle of the message again.

She uses her beauty as a weapon to ensnare men. She steals their money, lures them away from their families, and takes advantage of them until they are broken and ruined, both financially and emotionally. She even drives many of them to the point where they take their own lives.

Hmm. Human or not, this woman seemed to deserve what she had coming to her. Very well.

He would take the mission. He had to kill someone anyway. It might as well be her.

"Has he responded yet?" the hooded figure inquired in a low tone.

"Not yet," her companion replied.

The first figure shifted her feet restlessly. "So, is that good or bad?"

Her companion nodded, then seemed to realize the gesture couldn't be seen in the dark. "It means he has accepted the job. Had he rejected it, he would have returned the payment."

The first figure grinned in satisfaction. "Then our business here is done."

Isa couldn't sleep. She sighed and flopped her arm over her head, opening her eyes and glaring at the fire in the fireplace as though it were somehow at fault. Images flooded her mind, nagging at her, pestering her like, like... A picture of her old governess's face on the body of a mosquito buzzing around the room popped into her head. Like that. Isa giggled.

She leaned up and fluffed her pillow, then flipped onto her side, her cheek resting on her hand amidst the feathery softness. At least she was warm and comfortable. She squeezed her eyes shut and attempted to banish Lord Alistair's stricken visage from her overactive memories. However, every time it faded away, it was immediately replaced by that of Lord

Williams or Princess Nixa, or worse, the mysterious elf.

Why was life so complicated? *No*, she thought; she couldn't complain. She knew that most women in Penningdon would give anything to change places with her. She appeared to have it all. And to be honest, she did. Her life was very good.

She tried to focus on the positives. She had wealth, beauty, privilege. Pretty much anything she wanted, she could have. So, why wasn't she happy? Did she have a victim mentality? Was she too entitled? Spoiled? She sighed. What was wrong with her?

Isa flopped over onto her back, legs straight and stiff. She had to do something. She couldn't just lie there tossing and turning all night.

She finally gave up and rolled out of bed. Using the light of the full moon that streamed through the window, she made her way to her bathing chamber. She pulled a small green bottle from the cabinet and gripped it tightly.

This green bottle was the only thing that kept her from going insane after she witnessed her father being slaughtered by elven warriors. The nightmares that followed had threatened to undo her. She'd been taking the medicine periodically ever since.

She wandered over to her window and gazed up at the stars. Her light chemise fluttered against her legs as a gentle breeze slipped into the room. The universe was so vast. The largeness of it—its distance—made her feel as if she were floating through emptiness with nothing left of the real world except the bedroom in which she stood. Her imagination birthed within her a desire to spread her arms, lift her feet from the ground, and soar out into that infinite, unknown domain inhabited only by the heavenly bodies.

Isa shut her eyes and imagined. This time, it wasn't the face of a man or a rival that invaded her peace. It was the face of a little girl who had come into the poor hospital a few days ago. She had been beaten by an abusive father. Isa and Carrie had managed to help the girl and her mother escape. They had provided her with money and safe passage to Ravendall where they could start a new life.

No, things weren't perfect for her, but they were worse for many others. Much worse. She needed to rise above her self-pity and focus on more important things. But first, she had to rest.

Isa took the top off the green bottle and considered it. The medicine did help her sleep, but she hated using it because it worked too well. She felt uneasy being so helpless under its deep influence. But she needed something tonight. Her mind was in such a whirl; she wouldn't get any rest without it. She drank only a small portion of the potion and quickly returned to bed before it began to take effect. Her mind sank into darkness within moments, and she knew no more.

The open window mystified Thallan. Other than Lord Byron with his excess of guards, humans were so careless, as if the simple fact that a room existed on the third floor made it safe from intruders. Perhaps it did. From human intruders.

Landing soundlessly on the soft, plush rug, Thallan took a moment to survey the room. Surprisingly tastefully furnished, for a human abode, it still had too many feminine accoutrements to appeal to him. But, he figured, it could strike the right tone with the mortal men she pursued. He wondered if this was where she brought her targets before she bled them dry, figuratively, of course. If so, it seemed only fitting that this be where he would bleed her dry, literally.

The familiar urge to kill built as a dull ache spread through his head. Breathing deeply to slow its progress, he glared at the pale figures floating around him—the visible sign of his curse that only he could see. He didn't know who or what they were. The ghosts, perhaps, of those he had killed before. They certainly wore their faces. But he didn't believe in ghosts.

No, more likely, it was evil spirits taking on their likeness, sent by the goblin mage to plague him. The goblin was the one to condemn him to this cursed existence, and they had appeared shortly after his demise. It didn't seem like a stretch to link the two.

He had learned long ago that it was pointless to rage at them, to order them to leave him be. Always with him, their voices could only be silenced by visiting down death on his victims. Then, and only then, would they give him any peace, but even then, they did not vanish from sight.

As long as he was under the curse, he would never be alone. For death and the dead always followed him, pushed him, urged him on wherever he went. They were his constant companions.

Thallan moved through the moonbeams like a ghost himself. Like Death incarnate. He felt his mind slipping into the numbness that regularly accompanied these nightly activities. He allowed his emotions to fade away like smoke in the wind. It was better that way.

He did not enjoy the killing, but he didn't mind it, either. He was a warrior. He had brought an early end to many throughout his life. This was different, however. Assassinating a helpless female while she lay sleeping... His warrior honor instinctively recoiled from that. The lack of emotions would be a boon this night.

Thallan eased towards the bed, silently pulling his dagger from its sheath. A thin, white curtain hung from the bed's canopy, hiding its occupant from view. Thallan moved slowly and silently as he pulled back the material, revealing the lady whose life he had come to extinguish.

For a moment, he stood frozen, staring at the beauty lying before him. Her hair fanned out on her pillow, framing the lovely, familiar face. Rage surged through him, shattering his emotional barrier like hot metal shatters ice. Other feelings, unfamiliar feelings, began to seep through the breach as well.

Why did it have to be her?

The thought confused him. Why did it matter? He owed her no debt. He had not asked for her assistance. He had simply taken what she'd freely offered. He made no promises in return. She knew what he was, and she knew he was a killer. His bloody clothes and the dagger in his thigh hinted at no other conclusion. Still, why did it have to be her?

And why had she done it?

He peered at her intently, wishing her eyes were open so he could get a glimpse into her soul. Why had she helped an elf assassin when she so clearly despised his people? He hated not knowing. Unsolved puzzles such as this had a way of sticking with a person and plaguing them for years.

He actually considered waking her and asking, but the ache in his head began throbbing more insistently. He had a job to do. He couldn't let curiosity or any of these other strange feelings distract him from his task.

Already, his emotions began to fade again as the magic gained strength. Anger was the last to go, and it held on, stubbornly, like a miser holding on to his gold. How dare this girl affect him this way! She was a human and an evil, conniving one at that.

He positioned his dagger against her throat. Very well, he had always believed in being honest with himself. He would acknowledge that her kindness and beauty had impacted him for a moment, even though he had believed himself above such things. She had temporarily gained the upper hand in their strange battle. He noted the fact and filed it away as something to be wary of in the future. But the moment had passed. He had regained control. This was the last time she would have such an effect on a man.

He softly placed his hand against her cheek, taking care not to awaken her, anchoring her head in place to ensure a swift, clean cut if she tried to move. He would prefer to not bring her any pain as she died.

That was the least he could do.

That was the most he could do.

Her long, brown tresses felt like silk against his skin. Without thought, he lifted his hand, letting the strands fall through his fingers. Suddenly aware of what he did, he growled and tightened his fist around the locks, again being careful not to awaken her.

He glared down into her slumbering face. His breath came out hard in sharp bursts of anger that, again, broke through the haze of the magic. What was it about this girl? He had seen beautiful women before, plenty of them. He had been treated kindly before. By elves. What was it about this human that struck him so? How was her mere presence enough to disrupt the iron hold of the spell that bound him?

Staring at her, lying there so peacefully in the moonlight, an answer came to him. He understood what had stayed his hand. The girl looked so innocent, so pure. He knew what the letter had said, and it was possibly even true. He snorted. It could so easily be true, but seeing her like this... Remembering what she had done for him... She didn't appear to fit the description.

That was probably what made her schemes so effective. She looked and acted like a paragon of virtue. Somehow, though, he felt as if it were real. As if she were real—her actions and motives and intentions all agreeing and coming from a truly kind heart. Not done to manipulate or mislead.

Her behavior that night had certainly appeared genuine. She had nothing to gain by helping him and quite a bit to lose. He didn't trust beauty, but he did trust how people reacted when they were frightened or faced someone they despised. Fear and hate tended to reveal the tenor of a person's soul.

Thallan released his hold on her hair and leaned away, his eyes never leaving her face. He couldn't do it. His head was pounding with the need to kill, but he couldn't do it. He embraced the pain and thought. He only had a short time before his brain grew too foggy with the urge, and he lost control. He would go on a mindless rampage if he didn't kill someone soon. He needed to decide what to do and then do it quickly.

While he couldn't kill her, he couldn't leave her behind either. Not only would it damage his reputation and hurt his business, but the one who sent the contract would simply hire someone else. She would die anyway. There was no other option. He would have to take her with him. He groaned. This stupid, troublesome human was making his life difficult.

He touched her arm gently to see if she would wake. Removing her while she slept would be the most expedient course of action. If she tried to scream or fight him, it would slow him down. It would certainly be inconvenient for her to awaken in the middle of town. He would wake her now and then knock her out again.

When she didn't move at his gentle prodding, he shook her more roughly. He snorted when she didn't respond to that either. *Humans,* he thought. If she could sleep through that, she would sleep until he had her safely away.

Thallan pulled back the covers and slid his arms under her, slowly lifting her from the bed. Her body felt so small and fragile—and so soft. Were all humans females like this? If so, how did they survive in the hard, cruel world of men?

The scent of lavender drifted up to caress his nose, and the gentle pressure of her head resting against his heart sent a strange sensation surging up inside of him. He felt almost protective of this lady he had come to kill.

How odd.

And how odd that the magic would allow him to feel it. Was it because she was a woman? Could it be something more significant? Was it possible that she might be the one? She certainly fit the criteria. As he watched her sleep so peacefully in the arms of a killer, he realized that he wouldn't mind if she were.

As if that thought reanimated the curse, the phantoms that had faded with his musings began to wildly reassert their presence. They swarmed around him like angry bees, demanding his attention. The urge to end life filled him with a strength he had never felt from it before. Thankfully, his mind was still clear. The frenzy had not yet overtaken him.

Thallan pressed her to his chest and locked his arm muscles in place so they wouldn't betray his will and dash her to the floor. Maneuvering through the open window, he jumped lightly to the ground and took off at a speed that strained even his elven endurance.

As he sped through the shadows of the city, he used his elven water magic to surround them with a mist, further concealing their flight. To the few witnesses who did see them, he appeared more phantom than man. None were brave enough to risk his ghostly wrath to save the woman he was apparently abducting. Nor would they have had time to try if they had found the courage. He was gone in the blink of an eye.

The pounding in his head quickly grew more potent, and his arms tightened around their delicate burden. She would likely have bruises in the morning, but it couldn't be helped considering the alternative. He had to hold on just a little longer. Tearing through the forest at an inhuman speed, he finally reached the old, abandoned manor that had become his home. He kicked at the door until a beautiful elven woman jerked it open.

"Take her," he snapped, thrusting the girl into the elf's arms.

The woman instinctively caught her just before Thallan turned and vanished back into the surrounding trees. She glanced down at the girl, perplexed.

This was strange.

"Balin," she called, heading inside the house.

A tall, elven man with long blonde hair and a lean, muscular build appeared at the top of the stairs.

"Look," she said, nodding down at her load. She raised her arms as if presenting him with a gift. "A girl," she squealed excitedly.

Balin's face crumpled into a frown. "That's impossible, Ramona." He sniffed the air, and his eyes flashed dangerously. "She's human," he spat.

Ramona curled away from him, recognizing the glint in his eyes.

"Of course, she's human. She has to be. Don't you see? She could break the curse."

The man wrinkled his nose in distaste. "But she's human."

"She is not to be harmed," replied Ramona sternly.

Balin stepped closer to her and bent down threateningly over the girl. "Who's to say she isn't?"

Ramona rolled her eyes and swung her foot out to kick his shin. "Stop getting in my face." The man stepped back but didn't soften the scowl that marred his features.

"Prince Thallan brought her home and handed her over to me. She is not to be harmed," she repeated and strolled past him up the stairs.

Balin watched her go and smiled. Oh, how he loved that infuriating woman. He followed after his mate quickly. If Prince Thallan had brought this human to the house, there must be a reason. Very well, he would not harm her— unless instructed otherwise. He *would* watch her closely, though, for humans couldn't be trusted.

⚘⚘⚘

The daylight streaming through the window roused Isa from her deep, dreamless sleep. It penetrated the thin layer of her eyelids, and she turned her face from the offending rays. Yawning, she stretched her arms over her head.

40

When her hands bumped into solid wood instead of the veil hanging from her canopy, she felt around for a bit before opening her eyes.

Isa glanced sharply at the unfamiliar surroundings. This was not her room. Cautiously, she sat up and scanned her memories, trying to understand where she was.

"You sleep like the dead," a deep voice said disapprovingly.

Her head snapped around toward the sound. Her breath caught in her throat, and her eyes widened. She felt her heart pounding in her chest, though, to be honest, that might not have been entirely due to fear.

A tall, breathtakingly handsome man leaned against the doorframe, his icy blue eyes boring into hers. His intimidating presence filled the room. He stared at her, his muscular arms crossed over his chest, like he couldn't decide if he wanted to study Isa like a science experiment or save himself a lot of trouble and just dispose of her.

She opened her mouth to scream. He was beside her in an instant, leaning over the bed, his calloused hand covering her mouth, pushing her back against the pillows. He narrowed his eyes at her and frowned.

"Is this any way to greet the man who saved your life?" he growled out at her. Tendrils of long, silver hair brushed her face as he leaned closer.

She gasped behind his hand. Power emanated from his perfect features. Danger seemed to radiate from every pore of his being. A strong arm braced itself on the bed, trapping her within the circle of his body. Terror shot through her. Terror, and something else that she refused to acknowledge.

Suddenly, his words penetrated the haze of her fear. She mumbled into his hand, and he removed it, allowing her to speak.

"What do you mean you saved my life?"

"I am an assassin." His deep voice rumbled in the silence of the room. The words sent shivers down her spine. "I was hired to kill you, and yet, you live."

"Kill me? Who hired you to kill me?" Her voice trembled as the words tumbled out.

He stared at her without answering, his face only inches away. His eyes bore into hers as if he were attempting to see into her very soul. Isa forgot how to breathe.

Finally, he narrowed his eyes and pushed himself away.

"That I can't tell you. I take contracts through an intermediary. I don't know who hires me."

She sucked in a deep breath and blinked a few times, slowly processing his words. She sat back up and reached for his arm, stopping and pulling her hand back just shy of touching him.

"Would the intermediary be able to tell you if you asked?"

"Yes. But I'm not going to ask. I owe you no favors. Any debt that may have existed between us has now been paid."

He spun away from her and headed to the door.

"Wait."

He stopped but didn't turn.

"Thank you for not killing me."

The man looked back at her, a somewhat puzzled expression on his face. "You're welcome, human."

She studied him more closely. "You're not human?"

"Is that all?" he asked gruffly.

"No. Wait. What's going to happen to me now?"

"For the time being, you will stay here. If you are still alive after some time has passed... We'll see."

"What do you mean if I'm still alive? Are you going to kill me after all?"

"That depends on how much you annoy me with your incessant questioning."

Isa ignored that remark. "But I need to get home. Everyone will be so worried about me."

"Everyone except the person who wants you dead. Do you think they'll be happy to see you? What do you think will happen when they realize you are still alive? The next assassin might not be as generous as I am." He jerked the door open. "For now, you will stay here."

Isa fell back against her pillows when he left, her hand resting against her rapidly beating heart. *Oh my!* she thought.

Chapter 3

Isa pushed the last book back into place on the bookshelf, disappointed that none of them had opened a secret door. She glanced around the room, looking for other possibilities. Moving to the window, she tried, for the third time, to open it. No luck.

A sharp 'click' drew her attention to the door. Someone had unlocked it. Was the man back? Maybe she could surprise him and knock him out with the fireplace poker. Before she could act on that ludicrous notion, the door swung open.

She blinked in surprise when a beautiful woman walked in carrying a tray laden with food. Isa's stomach growled. She hadn't realized she was hungry until the smell of freshly baked bread and savory meat hit her nose.

"Good morning, human," the woman said pleasantly, setting the tray on the table. "You must be hungry."

There was that word again. Human.

The woman wiped her hands on her apron and greeted Isa with a friendly smile.

"I'm Ramona. I do all the cooking and cleaning around here."

Isa stood by the window, her hand still resting on the latch. She quickly lowered it.

"I'm Isabella," she replied hesitantly, not wanting to be rude to the friendly girl.

"Hello, Isabella. Why don't you have a seat, and I'll pour you something to drink." Isa warily watched her pick up the pitcher and fill a goblet with its contents. The clear liquid appeared innocuous enough, but...

Ramona placed it, along with a plate and silverware, in front of one of the chairs. Isa still didn't move. The man she had met that morning had made no secret of the fact he was a killer. And he had made no promises to let her live. The opposite, in fact. How could she trust anything in his house?

After Ramona had laid everything out, she turned and looked at their prisoner.

"Are you not hungry after all?"

Isa's stomach took that moment to growl again, and she blushed at the loud noise.

Ramona quirked a brow. "So, still hungry then. Do you not like bread, cheese, or venison? Some fruit, perhaps?" She placed a bowl of strawberries next to the plate.

Isa glanced at the food skeptically.

Ramona laughed, finally understanding. "Ah, you think it's poisoned."

Isa shrugged. "How can I be sure that it's not?"

"Two ways," the woman said, picking up the loaf of bread and tearing off a piece. Without another word, she stuck it in her mouth and chewed it, a contented smile spreading across her face.

"And the other way?" Isa asked when Ramona swallowed down the mouthful. After all, if they *weren't* human, what would poison her might not hurt them.

Ramona laughed again. "Did you see the man who brought you here? I know he visited you this morning. If he wanted you dead, do you really think he would poison you?"

Isa, of course, couldn't argue with that logic, and she was hungry. She hurried over to the table and sat down, attempting not to let her hunger overcome her manners as she quickly consumed the delicious food.

While Isa ate, Ramona opened a door on the corner wall to reveal a closet filled with a rainbow of beautiful gowns.

"Now, we need to find you something more appropriate to wear," she said. "You can't continue running around in that nightgown. It isn't proper, especially if Thallan continues to visit you." She began sifting through the dresses, pulling some out and hanging them on a different rack and moving others to the back. Isa sat there and watched her, munching contentedly on her meal.

"Who is Thallan?" she asked between mouthfuls.

"He was to be your assassin, but now he is your abductor, your captor—the one who is holding you prisoner."

Isa rolled her eyes. "I guessed that. I mean, who is he? Where does he come from? He called me human, too. Is he not human?"

Ramona continued her perusal of the gowns. "Those are a lot of questions," she said from inside the small room.

"Okay," said Isa with a slight huff, "will you answer just the last one, then?"

"And what was the last one?"

Isa growled under her breath. She was sure Ramona knew exactly which question she meant.

"Is he human?"

Ramona leaned back and peered at Isa through the doorway. She hesitated for a moment before she answered. "No."

Isa's breath caught, and her hands began to tremble. Of course, he wasn't. She had already suspected, but she had hoped. Now, hearing it stated so clearly... If he wasn't human, with the way he looked, his size, his coloring, there was only one thing he could be.

"Then what is he?" she asked nervously, needing her guess to be wrong.

"He's an elf. We're elves," said the woman, pulling back her long, thick hair to reveal her pointed ears.

A sob wracked Isa's body. Memories of watching elven warriors slaughter her father flashed through her mind. She squeezed her eyes tightly, trying to shut out the scenes of brutality. They had been playing with him. They could have killed him instantly, but they didn't. They drug it out, chopping him up, bit by bit, piece by piece.

Bile rose in her throat as visions of blood and gore and death tore through the darkness behind her eyes. She tried to push the thoughts away, but she couldn't this time. They overwhelmed her. Consumed her.

She felt Ramona's hand on her shoulder. The elf was saying something, but the words didn't pierce the fog in her head. She shrugged the hand off and ran toward the bed, throwing herself on the covers. Trembles shook her frame, and she broke down into tears. She didn't even hear the door softly closing behind Ramona as the elf left her alone to her grief.

Thallan and Balin circled each other in the wooded clearing, swords in hand. The clang of steel against steel was all that broke the silence of the forest. Thallan could see the unasked question floating in his friend's eyes like foam over a stormy sea.

He didn't like it.

He wasn't sure how to respond if the question was voiced, for he wasn't sure he completely understood his actions himself.

Finally, Balin broke the silence. "What were you thinking, Thallan?"

Thallan lunged in, aiming for his friend's neck. Balin blocked the sword with his own. Thallen swung his other blade toward Balin's stomach. His opponent only barely managed to dodge in time. Balin scowled.

"I don't know what you mean," replied Thallan dismissively.

"You know exactly what I mean. You brought a human female home with you last night." Balin's sword descended toward Thallen's head with incredible force. "Tell me why."

Thallan raised both his blades to block the weapon's descent.

"I couldn't kill her," he reluctantly admitted.

Balin narrowed his eyes, his grip on the sword tightening. "She was marked for death. What made you spare her?"

Thallan sighed and let the points of his blades drop to the ground. He stepped away from Balin and turned to look out over the clearing to the many trees beyond. "I couldn't do it. She helped me the other night when I was injured—the night I didn't return."

"She's the one?"

Thallan nodded.

"You said she offered. You didn't ask. You owe her nothing for that."

Thallan shrugged. "I don't believe she did the things the letter accused her of doing."

"You are the executioner, not the judge. Your job is to kill, not to decide if the person is worthy of death."

"Why? No court passes sentence on my victims. They are chosen simply because someone wants them dead. Who's to say the person demanding their death is any better than my victims are? Most likely, they are worse if they don't hesitate to contract an assassin. At the very least, they are cowardly for not completing the work themselves. I may be forced to kill, but that doesn't mean I have to become a tool to be used by unscrupulous humans. Why should I not have a say in whose light I extinguish?"

"You're right, but that doesn't explain why you spared this one. Just because she helped you doesn't mean she is innocent of the accusations made against her. It's possible that she did it to put you in her debt."

"I don't believe so. She looked so...innocent that night—so sweet and harmless, so vulnerable."

"Beauty does not always equate with innocence. You know that."

Thallan frowned. "I know that." He shook his head in frustration. He couldn't explain it. Balin seemed to sense his growing agitation.

He was silent for a moment, watching his friend carefully. "She's still a human."

Thallan nodded, his eyes roaming the clearing. "I know, but I don't think she's done anything wrong. I don't believe she deserves death. If I discover otherwise, I can always rectify the situation."

Balin stepped closer, the edge to his voice softening. "And what will you do with her now?"

Thallan said nothing, his gaze still fixed on the trees.

Balin laid a hand on his friend's shoulder. "We can't keep her here forever, Thallan."

Thallan turned to face his friend. "I trust your judgment. What do you think I should do?"

"Maybe you could find a way to help her disappear, to start a new life far away from here."

"There's some merit to that idea, but it would have to been done carefully, or whoever put the contract out on her might find her again."

"We could always fake her death," suggested Balin.

Thallan nodded. "If it came to that."

Balin squeezed his shoulder. "We can talk about it later if you wish. For now, let's finish our practice."

Thallan nodded and turned to face his friend. He raised his sword and swirled around him in a deadly dance. The silence between them was comfortable now, the tension gone.

Isa still lay across the bed, but she had cried herself out. For the present, at least. Now, she just felt numb. Empty.

She didn't know how long she had slept after her emotions had drained away into darkness, but the sky outside her window twinkled with stars. A fire roared in her fireplace, and a new tray of food sat on her table, casting enticing aromas out into the room.

Ramona had been back.

Isa was grateful that the elf woman had not woken her. Ramona had shown nothing but kindness to her. Isa didn't want kindness from an elf right now. She wanted to hold onto her anger. It would be a betrayal of her father to allow herself to feel any differently.

But her anger was slow to come. It almost didn't seem worth the effort. She had used up all of her emotions in her earlier outburst. She halfheartedly searched through the barrenness of her spirit in an attempt to dredge up some feeling—some passion, negative or positive.

Thallan. Wasn't that the name Ramona had used for the elf assassin who had captured her? Why had he not killed her? It must be because she had helped him when he was injured, for it had to be the same man. Elves didn't frequent Penningdon, and the likelihood that two killer elves were there now was slim.

She had heard that elves were immortal and that they didn't age like humans did. If that were true, Thallan could be decades old. Centuries old, even. He could even be one of the elf warriors who had killed her father.

Isa felt a spark of anger materializing in her core. Even if he weren't, he had clearly killed many humans. He was covered in blood when she found him that night. He had admitted to being an assassin. Assassins were killers for hire who worked for whomever would pay them. She didn't need any more proof that he was evil. He had escaped her once. He wouldn't escape her again.

Determination grew alongside her simmering thirst for vengeance. No, not vengeance. She wanted revenge. Otherwise, she wouldn't be so eager to deal it out on someone who may not have been involved. She didn't care. He was an elf warrior. He was the same.

Isa jumped out of bed and looked around the room. First, she would need to get dressed. She couldn't very well walk through town in her chemise. She went to the closet and examined the gowns. They were all so long. Maybe she could pin one up.

Grabbing a simple forest green dress, Isa quickly slipped it on. It was a bit snug across the chest and a tad loose around the waist, but that wasn't a problem. The problem was that it bunched around her feet like a mossy knoll.

Clearly, this dress belonged to an elf. Ramona, most likely. No human she knew had such a tall, slender build as this, but Ramona did. She spotted a pair of scissors lying in a sewing kit on one of the shelves and felt only a twinge of remorse as she cut the excess fabric from the gown. Tucking the scissors into her waistband, she walked over to the table and stuck a slice of cheese in her mouth while she worked on a plan.

She had to find some way out of there. She tried the doorknob. She wan't really expecting anything, so she wasn't too disappointed to discover it was locked. She had already searched the room for other ways out and found nothing. What other options were there?

She could wait behind the door for someone to come and then hit them over the head with something. Could she take Thallan down that way? Probably not. But if Ramona came in with her hands full with the breakfast tray, she might be able to surprise her. She didn't like the idea of hurting the girl, but Ramona *was* an elf, and she *was* working with the assassin, so she wasn't completely guiltless.

Isa sighed. Who was she kidding? She didn't know how to knock someone out. Where did you hit them? On the top of the head? At the base of the skull? And how hard should you hit them? She didn't want to kill anyone, especially not Ramona. Thallan, maybe, but she didn't see that happening.

Besides, morning would be too late. She needed to get out while it was still dark. If Thallan went on his killing sprees every night, he could be in town right now. This might be her only chance. She needed to find some other way out.

Isa bent down and peered through the keyhole. Sometimes, people left the key in. If she could push it out somehow and make it drop

53

onto something... But there was no key there. Frustrated, she scanned the room.

An idea wiggled its way into her consciousness. Five-fingered Willie had once told her how he had picked a lock. She had been bandaging a stab wound he had received from the owner of the door at the time. She had never tried it, but it didn't sound difficult. She just needed something to use.

She rummaged through the sewing kit but found nothing that seemed to fit the description of his tools. Searching through the other boxes on the shelves, she came across a jewelry chest. She shifted through the beautiful gold and silver and gemstones without taking the time to appreciate their breathtaking magnificence.

At the bottom of the box, she found two lovely emerald hair ornaments, both of which were attached to bobby pins. That might suffice. Kneeling before the door, Isa got to work. She tried and failed and tried and failed and tried and failed again. At one point, she gave up and circled the room looking for another solution but ended up back at the door, hairpins in hand.

Finally, after what felt like hours, she heard a soft click. She scrambled to her feet. Throwing open the door, she started to rush out before she realized she wasn't wearing any shoes. With a frustrated growl, she once again rummaged through the closet.

She couldn't find any at all. Did elf women not wear shoes, or did Ramona have another closet in her room where she kept her clothes? That would make more sense. They didn't expect Isa to leave the room, so there would be no need to supply her with footwear.

For a moment, she felt a wave of despair overcome her. She couldn't go running through the forest in the middle of the night without any shoes. But she couldn't stay there either. Scanning the closet again, Isa spotted a row of scarves. Grabbing the sturdiest-looking ones, she wrapped them around her feet and tied them tightly. She wouldn't win any fashion awards, and they might fall off before she made it to town, but they were better than nothing. She patted the scissors still tucked into her belt to ensure they were secure and quietly snuck down the corridor.

Could she be the one to break the curse? Thallan asked himself for the hundredth time. She had helped him despite her hatred of his kind, so it was possible she could develop feelings for him, eventually. Wasn't it? But love was a strong emotion and greatly distanced from hate. Or was it?

Storybooks often connected them—two powerful passions that bled together, intertwined, morphed back and forth. He could understand how passionate anger could shift to passionate lust. However, anger did not possess the soul-deep, steadfast intensity of hate. Nor did lust require the profound understanding of a person and the willingness to sacrifice our own needs and desires for them. Those, more than physical attraction alone, constituted the bond of love.

These two were not always exhibited through the fiery passion that created such an easy bridge over the gulf that separated them. Was there even a path from one to the other? If so, could they find it?

Even for the sake of his future, he wasn't sure he could so effortlessly put aside his disdain for her race. The feelings were too entrenched and had been for too long to be lightly cast aside. But, for the sake of that future, he could try. He would begin by checking on her before he retired for the night.

Thallan sensed that something was wrong as soon as he entered her corridor. The air carried a faint scent of her passing. He hurried to her room and slung the door open. How had she gotten out? Had Ramona forgotten to lock it?

His eyes landed on the two emerald hairpins that lay discarded by the entrance. What a clever girl. He had underestimated her.

Thallan burst from the manor and tore into the forest—the opposite direction from town. Not too clever, it seems. Her trail was easy enough to follow even in the dim light. He would catch her soon.

Even though his blood lust had dissipated with the job he had just completed, he still acknowledged that he would have to kill the girl. He felt like he was beginning to understand her, and he was confident that if he returned her to the manor alive, she would try again. And with the threat to her life still a reality, there could only be one purpose for her flight. She wanted to turn him in.

He couldn't risk her putting the lives of Ramona and Balin in danger by bringing the king's guard down upon them, even if the eventuality was highly unlikely. It was a pity, though. He would have to find some other way to break the curse.

The pain in Isa's side had become almost unbearable, but she didn't dare stop. The stars were already beginning to fade. Morning would arrive soon. If Thallan had not already returned to the manor, he would before long. He could, even now, be searching for her.

She had been too rash. She should have waited. She could have left earlier, right after Thallan headed into town if she'd postponed it to tomorrow night. She could have planned better. She might could have even gotten some information about their location from Ramona. And some shoes.

The scarves flopped uselessly around her feet. She just kicked them off instead of retying them again. She didn't have time for this. Forest debris bit into her soles as she ran over the littered ground. She embraced the pain. It was the punishment for her rash stupidity, and she accepted it.

Isa heard a roaring up ahead and rushed toward it. Water was good. She could use it to disguise her trail. But when she grew closer, her enthusiasm waned. The stream was too wide, and the water rushed too wildly and quickly for her to even imagine crossing it. She would have to change directions. That didn't matter a great deal, though, since she had no idea where she was going. She turned and headed downstream.

There was no warning. No rustling of leaves. No broken twigs. Not that any of that could be heard over her stampeding gait, anyway. But she would have expected some advance notice.

There was nothing.

Thallan simply appeared before her. She skidded to a stop and raised her eyes sheepishly to meet his. Why did his iron gaze fill her with guilt? She had done nothing wrong. He was the monster. She wanted to do the right thing and turn him in, then return to her own life.

A small voice in the back of her mind wondered how long she would live once she did. Would another assassin be dispatched? She pressed her lips together. That didn't matter. He had to be turned in.

"Tell me this." Thallan's voice was as hard as steel. "Do you care nothing for what will become of Ramona?"

His question surprised her. "What do you mean?"

"When you bring the soldiers down on us, what do you think they'll do to her?"

Isa didn't reply. She hadn't wanted to dwell on that unfortunate aspect of her plan. She stubbornly straightened her back, raised her chin, and stood as tall as her five-foot, four-inch frame would allow. He glared down at her, unimpressed.

"Are you here to take me back or to kill me?"

"To kill you. I can't have you threatening the safety of my friends this way." He pulled a sword from its scabbard.

Isa gulped. "I see. What if I promised never to escape again?"

"I wouldn't believe you, and the lie would destroy any respect you have previously earned from me. For a lie it would be, would it not?"

"Yes," she admitted reluctantly.

He acknowledged her honesty with a nod.

58

Isa took a deep breath, struggling to hold at bay the panic that threatened to cloud her thinking. What could she do? Her eyes darted around the forest. How could she escape? The roar of the river called to her. She could never survive its waters, could she?

"Have you made peace with your coming demise?"

She turned back to the assassin. "No." She saw no point in lying to the man.

"As I said, I have some little respect for you. Because of that, I will grant you a quick, painless ending."

"I would prefer no ending at all."

He shook his head. "That I cannot do."

"Then my choices seem clear—perish by your sword or risk death by plunging myself into these rapids."

"It matters not to me. The river will kill you as surely as I will."

"Maybe not." Isa stared into the raging stream and considered it critically. She was a good swimmer, but that would make little difference in these tumultuous waters. However, of her two options, this was the only one that offered her any hope of survival, small though it may be.

"I'll take my chances with nature. Perhaps the Maker will smile down on me."

"As you wish." Thallan slid his blade into place and crossed his arms over his chest. He leaned back against a tree and waited, watching her curiously.

It was the wisest option if she wanted to live, but did she have the courage to do it? Even in the improbable event that she did survive, she would emerge broken and bruised. It would be a painful experience. A painful death. She had exhibited admirable degrees of bravery in other encounters with him, but throwing yourself to the mercy of the icy depths would only be done lightly by a fool. And she was no fool.

Perhaps he should save her from the anguish she was so clearly experiencing by taking off her head now while her back was turned. It would be a much easier end than what she would receive at the merciless hands of the river. He meant it when he said he didn't want to bring her any pain. Even if she was a human.

Before he could decide, she waded into the violent water. It swept her legs out from under her almost immediately, and she disappeared beneath the churning rapids. Thallan saw her resurface a few yards downstream and ran along the bank, following her as she bobbed and sank and surfaced, only to repeat the cycle several times.

He knew she would die there that day, for how could she survive? She was so small, so weak and fragile, even for a human. Yet, he couldn't walk away. He couldn't leave her to die alone. Something inside him wanted to be there for her. He wouldn't stop what had to happen, but he wouldn't allow her life to be extinguished without even a witness.

He followed her progress silently, stoically. He had expected her to give up shortly after she fell in, but she fought valiantly. Several times, she came close to rocks rising above the foam, and on a few of those occasions, she appeared to almost gain a hold. Only to lose it again.

At one point, he noticed she was gradually edging toward the far bank. The clever girl was swimming at an angle as she was hurled downstream. She had kept her head in the midst of the chaos.

Impressive.

He continued following her from the bank, then took to the trees when the forest grew too thick to easily navigate from the ground. She was successfully maneuvering closer to the shore. If she lived long enough, she might actually make it. He was surprised as the desire for her to survive suddenly welled up inside him.

Such a useless desire.

If she did survive, he would still have to kill her. It would seem almost tragic to do so after she had so courageously fought and defeated the raging river. Still, it must be.

She was beginning to tire. He could tell. The waters pulled her under more often, and she remained submerged for longer periods of time. It appeared that she wouldn't make it after all.

Thallan continued to run along the branches and jump from one to another, following the drowning girl. Looking ahead, he spotted a log that had fallen into the river, lying directly in her path. If the human could reach that alive, she might yet be saved.

He watched as the ruthless waves viciously tossed about the pale, limp form as if they were reluctant to allow her the strength to part from them when the opportunity came. Finally, her bruised body crashed into the log. For a moment, it appeared as though she would be pulled underneath it, but she managed to grab on. He was surprised by her tenacity.

Thallan felt a bit brutish watching a lady in clear distress and doing nothing to assist, but she had to die that day. It was the only way he could ensure the safety of his friends—short of leaving the kingdom, and he wouldn't do that for a mere human. He had his reasons for wanting to be there. If only the manor had a dungeon...

As Thallan watched her struggle to pull herself onto the log, conflicting emotions filled him. He felt pride in her for her triumphant victory. That such a weak, fragile being could conquer the mighty river was an accomplishment that couldn't exist without acknowledgment and praise.

However, he was also disappointed. How much easier it would have been on his conscience if the waters had taken her. He did not like the idea of destroying someone with such a powerful will. Someone who was prepared to risk her life for what she believed was right. Someone who choose the difficult, painful path to freedom over an easy death. She was stronger than he had given her credit for— not in body alone, but also in spirit, and that was what truly mattered.

She was a warrior.

A warrior worthy of respect.

His task was becoming increasingly distasteful. He just wanted it to be over with. If he'd had his bow with him, he would have shot her then, but he didn't.

The girl lay there for a while, draped over the sodden wood. He could see her chest moving with her deep breaths. Her dress clung to her like a second skin, and her soaked hair stuck to her face and neck. Her tiny feet hovered only inches from the water, the soles of which appeared unnaturally red, though Thallan couldn't see any details from that distance.

The human only lay there for a few moments before she lifted her head and looked around, searching for him, no doubt. She didn't see him. For she neglected to look up into the trees.

After a short struggle with her dress, which had twisted itself around her legs, she managed to scoot herself up the log and tumble off onto the dry ground. She pushed herself onto shaky legs and stumbled awkwardly away from the water, slowly disappearing into the surrounding trees.

Thallan sighed.

He rose from his squat and walked further out on the branch. Scanning the river, he searched for a narrow enough spot where he could cross. Seeing no possibilities nearby, he considered his options.

There was a good location upstream that they had passed early on, but the girl would most likely continue moving downstream since she surely would have deduced that that was the fastest way to civilization. It wouldn't take him long to catch up to her, even by going out of his way, but he didn't want to waste any more time. He would see what opportunities lay in the South.

Decision made, Thallan headed downstream.

Isa had no idea where she was. Her feet were cut and bloody. Her whole body was bruised and sore. Her legs felt like they would give out at any moment. But she had escaped her assassin.

He'd seemed so sure that she would perish in the river. He must have returned to the manor. She hadn't seen him anywhere nearby when she left the water. But there was also the possibility that he had gone downstream to wait for her body to wash up somewhere. So, she headed upstream through the forest.

She chastised herself for not paying better attention in her geography classes as a child, but she vaguely remembered learning about a small village on this side of the river. It hadn't appeared too far away on the map. Maybe if she headed in that direction, she would run into someone.

Thin rays of early morning sunlight forced their way down through the thick foliage to illuminate her path. She was thankful for this blessing. It allowed her to choose her steps more carefully. Even so, her poor feet were not spared further injury. The forest floor was just too harsh for her tender skin.

She winced as a sharp stick added its mark to her sole. She wished she hadn't been so hasty in discarding her scarves. She wished she had asked Ramona for some shoes. She wished she hadn't fallen asleep that day at Carrie's and had turned Thallan in to the guards then. That was what she wished most of all.

However, her practical nature never allowed her to get away with lying to herself. She knew she would be dead right now if she had summoned the guard while the assassin slept.

Probably.

Possibly.

The man had lost a good deal of blood. Surely, he wouldn't have been able to fight off the king's guard. Would he?

Well, she would most likely be dead either way. If the guard had managed to capture him, some other assassin would have come for her and killed her. If he had managed to escape, it's unlikely he would have let her live after that.

Why had he let her live? Was it just because she had helped him, or was there more to it? Whatever his motives, they clearly no longer held any sway since he seemed to have no problem killing her now.

Another sharp object pierced Isa's foot. The sudden pain caused her already weak legs to give out, and she sank to the ground. A tear of frustration and despair coursed its way down her cheek. She couldn't go on like this.

She took the scissors, which had miraculously held on through her wild flight in the forest and the chaos of the river, from her waistband and cut a length of fabric off the bottom of her gown. It was still a soggy mess. Wringing the water out over her aching foot, she cleaned it as well as she could and wrapped the material tightly, tying it in place. She felt a tad better after doing the same to her other foot.

Her experience with the scarves taught her that this solution wouldn't last long, but it was better than subjecting her poor appendages to additional damage. Besides, she had more dress she could cut off if needed.

The sun had long since passed overhead when Isa stopped for the third time to rewrap her feet. The gown fabric had proven to be considerably less durable than the scarves. Her face grew warm as she cut a strip of her dress off above the knees.

She had almost not done it. How was she to face any potential rescuers wearing such an indecent gown? Would potential rescuers actually rescue her if they saw her like this, or would she be in a whole different kind of trouble?

She had to take the risk. Her feet couldn't handle much more abuse. She wrapped her feet tightly and leaned back against a tree, allowing herself a moment to rest and think. She had been walking for hours without coming across any sign of civilization. Her stomach felt like it was eating itself, and her throat felt like sandpaper.

What was she going to do if she didn't find people soon? Would she have to sleep in the forest? Should she slow down and look around for some food? Surely, the assassin would have caught up to her by now if he were still looking. Maybe she should shift her efforts to finding a way to survive out here and somewhere to hide.

Did she dare retrace her steps? She felt confident she could find her way back to the elf's manor if she could get across the river. Not that she would go back to the manor, but she had a little more understanding of where things were now. She might have a better chance of finding the city if she started over. Oh, what should she do?

She leaned her head back and closed her eyes, taking a moment to listen to the birds and clear her mind. It was so peaceful there. No annoying men to pester you. No assassin trying to kill you. It might not be so bad living there.

She could build a little hut out of twigs and plant a small garden. Isa laughed at the ridiculous image. She prided herself on being adaptable, but she doubted she would excel at such a life.

With a deep breath, she pulled herself to her feet and took a couple of steps to test the ties of her makeshift shoes. She'd head back toward the river while continuing north, she decided. Her path had been growing steeper for a while, and she could see tall hills not too far away.

She might not remember much from her classes, but she did remember reading about a beautiful waterfall somewhere in this area. Perhaps the river would be easier to cross there. Once she made it back on the right side of the river, she shouldn't have as much trouble finding people.

The sun was beginning its slow descent by the time she heard the roaring of the falls. The sound was a welcome one—not only because it had been her destination but also because she felt weak with hunger and thirst. She hurried on, dropping to her knees beside the clear, calm water when she reached its banks.

It wasn't until after she had drunk her fill that she noticed the heavenly aroma of venison cooking over an open fire. Hesitantly, she turned her gaze toward the light of the blaze.

"Finally, the little mermaid deigns to acknowledge our presence."

Three men sat around the campfire. Dirt smeared their faces and mixed with oil to mat their dark hair.

"Huh?" replied the skinny man with long, lanky arms.

"He means the girl's finally looking at us," said the shorter one with a sparse beard decorating his chin.

"Oh."

They all turned toward her and smiled. Not a friendly smile. A predatory smile. A hungry smile. Isa had seen the like before—though not with such stained and rotted teeth behind them.

She quickly stood to her feet and began backing away, but the men were faster. They jumped up and closed her in with only the river at her back as an escape. She noticed their eyes gravitating toward her bare legs as they moved closer, and she unsuccessfully tried to pull her dress down to cover them.

"I wonder if the pretty mermaid would like to play with us," said the first man, who appeared to be their leader.

"I'd certainly like to play with her," replied the skinny one with a harsh laugh.

"I want to play with her first," insisted the short man.

"I saw her first. I get her first," demanded the leader.

Isa glanced over her shoulder at the river as they argued. Not again. She felt a twinge of fear at the thought of submersing herself a second time, but she definitely would prefer that to this current alternative. She'd even prefer the assassin to this alternative.

She turned and rushed into the river, but she wasn't quick enough. The leader grabbed her hair and pulled her back, jerking her off her feet. Isa fell, plunging under the water. She thrashed around until she felt the ground just beneath her. She felt her cloth shoes come undone and float away as she sat up, coughing and gasping for air. Frantically, she reached for the pair of scissors only to find them missing. The men laughed. The leader grabbed her arm and pulled her to her feet, dragging her onto the bank while the others advanced.

"We're going to have lots of fun with you, little mermaid."

Thallan was annoyed. He'd never had so much trouble assassinating anyone before. He followed the river south until he came across a wooden bridge standing next to a small village. Trees bordered the tiny town, so he concealed himself in their boughs and watched the people rushing around, seeing to their daily tasks.

He could cross now and be on his way, but with the sun shining so brightly, he couldn't make it over the bridge and to the tree line on the other side without being seen. He knew how he appeared. He'd had no opportunity to clean himself up and change before he'd taken off after the girl.

The evidence of his nightly activity still showed on his dark clothes. Also, his hood and face covering shrouded him in mystery and exuded an aura of danger. He looked exactly like the killer he was.

He could remove them. That might make him seem a little less threatening, but he doubted the sight of his elven ears would bring the people much more comfort. He could glamor them, but it wouldn't be as effective in the bright light of day, besides, that wouldn't solve the problem of his stained clothes.

There was always the option of killing them all. No witnesses would remain to tell of his presence. But such useless slaughter was not something he felt comfortable with. Not when there were other options.

Still, he couldn't have rumors spreading about a dangerous man, or worse, an elf, wandering around in the woods so close to his home. He didn't need the hassle that would come of people out searching for him.

It would be a while before the human's stumbling gait would carry her this far. He would wait and let her come to him. For now, he would hunt and break his fast. Thallan jumped down from the tree and headed deeper into the forest.

With his stomach satisfied by the rabbit he had killed and cooked a safe distance away, Thallan settled back on a tree branch and closed his eyes to rest.

The sun had already sunk below the tree line when he woke, refreshed. However, a sense of urgency descended upon him almost immediately when he began to feel the familiar stirrings of the curse. He had time. It was hours before the urge would prove unmanageable, but he still needed to take care of this business with the girl quickly. It had occupied too much of his time already.

Thallan scanned the village and felt confident that the girl had not yet arrived. Surely, news that an elf assassin was wandering their woods would cause chaos in the small town. Yet, everything appeared peaceful and serene.

A flash of concern emerged from somewhere deep inside him. She should have covered the distance by now. Something must have happened. He would have to look for her.

Shadows enveloped the wooden bridge, but not enough for him to cross over it unseen. Beneath the bridge, however, all had been plunged into darkness. The bridge's support beams would be simple enough to traverse. He just had to reach them without attracting notice.

If he wanted to leave now. What did it matter if something had happened to the girl? He was going to be the something that happened to her when he found her. Did another hour really matter?

Yes. He no longer felt satisfied with the thought of waiting until nightfall. Something drew him on, pulled him forward. It wasn't the curse this time. What was it? Concern for the human? Concern for his target? Surely not.

He *was* having a difficult time keeping her from his thoughts, though. But why wouldn't he? She had become such a problematic target. He would track her down, kill her, and then head into town to take care of his regular business. She would be out of his life and out of his mind—just another phantom for him to try to ignore.

A road separated the woods from the town. He would have to cross that first. Once he was on the other side, there was a scattering of bushes that would aid his passage to the bridge.

Only a few people remained outside walking about, but one was all that was needed to make his life much more difficult. He watched them carefully. When no eyes were turned his way, Thallan darted across the road and squatted down behind a bush.

Parting the thick foliage, he managed to open a wide enough space to peek through. Two women had stopped to talk in front of a door only a few yards away. They hadn't been facing him before, but now they were, and it didn't appear that they would be leaving any time soon.

He looked around for a distraction. The village well stood nearby, and a bucket sat on its rim. Reaching out with his water magic, Thallan felt for water in the pail, and when he found it, he pulled at the liquid, causing the bucket to fall to the ground with a clang. The women turned toward it, and Thallan crept on to the next bush, standing by the water's edge.

Slipping into the river, he grabbed one of the rough beams supporting the bridge and pulled himself across. With the deeper shadows cast by the trees on the other side, he had no trouble reaching the forest, and in just a few moments, he was running through the thick woods, searching for signs of the human's passing.

He saw no trace of her until he reached the spot where she had crawled out of the river. From there, it was easy enough to track her. Upstream.

So, the girl had traveled north. Was that more cleverness on her part or a sign of ignorance? Either way, it had worked to her advantage. Not that it would do her much good, but at least it had bought her a little more time on this earth.

Thallan followed her tracks closer to the hills. They headed toward the waterfall—prime hunting ground for poachers. A new urgency pushed his feet faster.

He heard them before he saw them. A burning rage filled him at the vile intentions of the human men. An urge to kill that had no connection to his curse rose in him, and he burst into the clearing, swords drawn.

Blood splattered over the girl's soaked gown as the head of the man holding her down flew off into the river. His body landed on top of her, and she gasped as she wiggled her way out from under it.

The other men didn't have time to run. Their screams died in their throats as two swords pierced their necks. They, too, fell to the earth in a rapidly growing red puddle.

Thallan wiped his blades on one of the men's clothes, then slid them back in place. He looked up to find the girl standing there stunned, a mix of relief and horror on her face. Suddenly, the fog seemed to lift from her eyes, and she turned and ran toward the small mountain.

Thallan crossed his arms and watched her go. Why did the girl insist on making this more difficult than it had to be? He took his time walking after her. It wasn't as if she could get away.

The human scrambled up the side of the steep hill, probably thinking she could cross the river more easily at the top. Or maybe she thought a legion of soldiers was up there waiting to rescue her. Or perhaps she expected to find a dragon she could quickly tame and sic on him. Who knew what that human could be thinking?

When she reached the top, Thallan ran the remaining distance and jumped from the edge to land lightly in front of her. The girl stopped at the bank of the river and glanced back down over the waterfall. The river was narrower there. She might have been able to cross it further upstream, but there was no way she could cross it there without going over the waterfall. Thallan was not about to let her move farther upstream.

It was time to end this.

The assassin removed his hood and lowered his face covering. As one warrior to another, he would allow her to look on him as he brought her life to an end.

"Come, human. Accept your fate. You know you cannot escape me."

"I know, but I'm not ready to give up yet." She glanced back down at the waterfall.

"You will only bring yourself more pain."

"It's my life. If I choose to bring pain into it, that's my decision."

"True, but it's not a very wise decision."

"Why not? Isn't pain, accompanied by hope, better than utter despair and hopelessness? Would *you* just give up and accept your fate if, with a little pain, you might be able to change it?"

Thallan was impressed with the insightfulness of her thoughts, but he couldn't ignore the flaw in her reasoning.

"I wouldn't, but you are assuming that by enduring the pain, you actually have a chance of changing your fate."

"I have hope; that's all."

"That's not enough." He pulled a dagger from his belt and stepped forward. "This will not hurt you at all. I promise."

"How can death not hurt?" Her lip trembled, and she took a hesitant step back. She was too close to the edge of the cliff. Despite her bravado and her earlier success, she wouldn't be able to survive a fall from that height, not with all the rocks below.

"I will plunge the dagger into the base of your skull. It will sever your spinal cord. You will feel nothing and die almost instantly. It is the best I can offer you."

She took another step backward, and he instinctively held out his hand to stop her. The foolish girl would fall if she weren't more careful.

"It isn't enough."

"Then what will you do to stop it?"

She took another step back, and the ground gave way beneath her feet. With a scream, she plummeted over the side.

Thallan let out a curse and ran to the edge. Peering over, he saw her hanging, clutching a tree root a few yards down. She wouldn't be able to hold on long. The spray from the waterfall would make the root slippery.

The stubborn girl was going to die slowly, a broken, mangled mess, once she hit those rocks. No, he wouldn't let her die like that. He'd still kill her to save her some pain, but she wouldn't escape it all like she would have if she'd just listened to him.

Thallan made his way back down the side of the steep hill, keeping an eye on the girl so he could watch and see where she landed when she lost her grip and fell. That's when he noticed the ledge jutting out from the cliff under the waterfall.

It was close enough to the girl that, with some help, she could reach it. But the ledge was narrow and slanted, and the rock would be too smooth and slippery with the wet for her to stand on with only her human balance to support her. Without another thought, Thallan ran back up the hill, leaped over the narrow river, and climbed back down on the other side. He eased himself across the face of the cliff, under the waterfall, until he reached the ledge.

Water pelted him, soaking him through. It was not a comfortable sensation. When he got into position, he used his magic to shield himself and remove the liquid from his clothes. He should just let the human fall and be done with it. But for some reason, he couldn't.

The girl's bare legs dangled only a couple of feet away. What had the crazy woman done to her dress? He forced his gaze away from her shapely legs only to be confronted with how her gown, what was left of it, stuck to her body, revealing her curves in a most tantalizing fashion.

He closed his eyes for a second to regain control of his wayward thoughts and focus on his task. With a deep, cleansing breath, he grabbed onto a protruding rock with one hand and reached out with the other. Leaning dangerously far over the edge, he managed to wrap his arm around the girl's legs.

She kicked at him and screamed.

"I'm trying to help you, you stubborn female. Hold still."

He waited a moment to see if she would obey, and when her thrashing stopped, he reached for her again. He wrapped his arms around her legs and called up.

"Let go. I have you."

"You'll drop me."

"You have my word that I won't."

The weight on his arm increased when she released her hold, and he pulled her toward him, slightly surprised that she'd trusted him. Her body slid down his as he lowered her to her feet, igniting a multitude of unwelcome sensations. Still, he held her against him, not quite ready to let her go. She hugged him tightly as well, shivering in his arms, whether from fear or cold, he couldn't tell. A bit reluctantly, he pulled his dagger from its sheath and reached around behind her.

She didn't fight him, though she must know what he was about to do. Instead, she clung to him more tightly, hiding her face in his shirt. He felt her tremble more violently against him, and he pulled her closer. He buried his face in her hair and whispered in her ear.

"I'm sorry."

Sweeping the wet locks over her shoulder, he moved the blade into position, pressing the tip against her neck. She let out a soft sob.

No screaming or begging.

No ridiculous promises.

No scandalous offers.

Just a single sob.

She had finally, bravely, accepted her fate. It saddened him, and though it was better this way, he felt a pang of regret and guilt that he was the one who had brought her to this point.

He stood there, gripping the knife tightly, willing his hand to finish the job, but his hand rebelled. It refused to move.

"Kill her. Kill her. Kill her." The phantoms danced around them, merging with the waterfall and passing through the face of the cliff behind him. "Kill her. Kill. Kill. Kill." Their chant grew louder and louder, like thunder rolling through his brain. Yet, his hand still refused to move.

"I can't let you tell anyone about us." Steel coated his words, yet a desperate plea for understanding weaved its way through the rigidity. "Ramona is not a warrior. She couldn't protect herself if the entire king's guard came after us, and we might not be able to protect her either."

"I like Ramona. I don't want to see her hurt." His shirt muffled Isa's voice, but Thallan still detected the sorrow in it.

"Yet, you will report us the first chance you get." It was not a question.

"Yes."

"Why?" He glanced down at her, and she lifted her face to meet his gaze.

"You're an assassin."

"There are many assassins in the city. Will you seek them all out?"

"No."

"Then why me?"

She looked away as if ashamed of the reality of her words. "You're an elf."

Thallan's lip curled up in a snarl. He glared down at the top of her head. Just like a human—hating someone simply because of their race.

"Kill. Kill. Kill." The voices, quieter now, still remained—still insisted. Though angry, he still resisted.

"Now we get the truth. You don't care that I'm an assassin. You only hate me because I'm an elf."

Isa looked up at him, her face wet with tears. The sight sent a disagreeable ripple through his body. He angrily shoved it aside.

"I do. I can't help it." Her eyes sought his and held them in an irresistible grip. "Why do you kill humans? Can you honestly say you don't hate us because of what we are?"

Thallan frowned, his anger seeping away. "No. I cannot honestly say that."

The girl gave him a faint smile. "I wish I could promise you I won't try to escape again, that I won't try to bring the guard down on you. I wish... I wish things could be different. But they aren't."

"You are a very strange human."

The girl laughed. "You are a very strange assassin."

No. Not usually. There was just something about this girl that stirred everything up inside him until his body would no longer obey his commands. Whatever was happening to him, he feared he would not be able to kill her. At least not then. The hand holding the dagger had already begun to inch away from her neck despite his strict instruction for it to move closer. And the arm holding her body onto the ledge inexplicably tightened its grip. He had to find another solution to their problem and quickly before she realized the power she held.

"I propose a compromise," he offered. "You say you have no ill will toward Ramona."

Isa nodded.

"Give me one month. During that time, I can fix things up so that Ramona can go away to safety. Also, your enemy should be less troubled by your disappearance by then. You can come out of hiding, and we can get you away as well. If you choose to go. If, at the end of the month, you still want to turn me in, I will give you a one-day head start. What do you think?"

"Really?" She tilted her head and considered him suspiciously.

"Really."

"And what is the alternative?"

Thallan pressed the blade into her neck, drawing a drop of blood. "Yes. Yes. Yes. Kill. Kill. Kill." The voices urged him on, but he ignored them.

The girl sucked in a sharp breath, her eyes opened wider.

"Would you even believe me if I agreed, considering the circumstances?"

Thallan studied her carefully. "I would, but just to ensure that you don't get any ideas later, know that while the guards may pose a threat to Ramona, they *don't* pose a threat to me. Nor to Ramona's mate, Balin. If anything were to happen to her, your end would *not* be painless. Nor would you die alone. We would find everyone you know and love, and they would all experience terrible and painful deaths along with you."

He felt a shudder rack her body.

"Fine. I agree to your temporary truce. One month. Thirty days. Starting today."

Thallan eased the blade away and sheathed it. Twisting slightly on the narrow ledge, he removed her arms from around his waist and twined them around his neck.

"You'll have to hold on tightly while I maneuver us out of here." The girl squeaked when he put his hands on her bottom and lifted her up. "Wrap your legs around my waist."

"What?!"

He frowned and gave her a hard stare. "Wrap your legs around my waist so you don't fall."

He gritted his teeth when she complied, hiding her very red face back in his shirt. Concentrating on his task, *not* the feeling of her body wrapped around him, he slipped an arm under her derriere to give her more support. Then, he carefully made his way across the slippery, narrow ledge back onto solid ground. However, when he reached the bank, he didn't release her.

"You can put me down now," said the girl, squirming in his arms.

He felt a strange reluctance to do so.

Interesting.

He was not blind to her charms, but she was a human. She should not be able to affect him that way. Still, his body rebelled against the orders of his mind. He grabbed her legs and swung them around so she lay in his arms.

"No," he replied, "You have wasted enough of my time already. I'm not going to waste more by moving at a snail's pace. I can travel much more quickly this way."

He pressed her snugly against his chest and took off through the forest at a run. He moved at a speed he rarely employed, desperation

81

pushing his legs forward. He had to get rid of this burden he carried, and soon. Even now, she filled his senses. He didn't dare glance down at her in her damp dress. The feeling of her bare legs against his hand and her arms around his neck were enough to drive him insane. He didn't think he could handle it if he added to that the vision of her lovely body.

What was wrong with him? Where was the strength of the curse when he needed it? True, it should have been satisfied with the deaths of those men, but it had asserted itself with her. Why hadn't it been stronger—more forceful? Why hadn't it made him do it so he could be done with all these unwelcome thoughts and desires?

In very little time, though it felt like an age, the manor came into view. The human tried to wriggle from his arms again when they reached the house, but he continued to hold her tightly. Thallan kicked at the door until Ramona opened it, shock filling her face at the sight.

"Take her," Thallan said, thrusting the girl into the elf's arms once again. "See to her injuries."

"Is this going to become a habit?" asked Ramona as she held her gently.

Thallan scowled. Without another word, he turned and ran.

Isa's whole body ached, and the disappointment of her failure the previous night weighed heavily on her. It was the first thing that came to mind when she awoke that morning. What was she to do? How could she ever succeed against him?

Even if the assassin gave her a head start, he was an elf. How could a mere human ever defeat an elf?

A soft knock sounded from the entrance to her chambers, but Isa ignored it. Ramona opened the door a crack and looked in.

"May I enter?" she asked.

"I can't stop you," Isa said, her voice muffled by the pillow in which she buried her face.

"Yes, you can," replied Ramona.

Isa snorted. "How? You're an elf. Elves are so much stronger and more powerful than humans. You can do anything you want to me, and I couldn't do anything to stop you."

Silence came from the doorway.

Ramona took a deep breath and entered the room. Isa huffed into her pillow when she heard her place another tray on the table.

"You could ask me to leave."

When Isa didn't reply, the elf walked over to the bed and sat beside her. She reached out tentatively and began patting Isa's back. At first, Isa stiffened at the touch, but she could tell there was nothing but friendliness in the gesture, even if it did come from an elf. She finally relaxed, and a tear snuck out to dampen the pillow.

"Thallan told us what happened last night. I'm sorry, he's forcing you to stay here against your will. But it is for the best. Whoever wanted you dead won't give up. You'll be in more danger if you leave."

It sounded like the assassin hadn't told her everything. That was fine with Isa. She didn't need the elf woman trying to persuade her to just leave peacefully after the month was over.

"That's not all that's bothering you, though, is it?" asked Ramona. "You've been upset ever since you learned we were elves."

Isa didn't respond.

"What happened to you? Why do you have this hatred for my people?"

Isa lay there in silence, images rushing through her head—horrible, violent images.

"They killed my father." The words tumbled out unbidden.

The elf didn't have to ask who. "I'm so sorry."

Isa sniffed. "There were four of them." She turned her head sideways so the pillow wouldn't obscure her words. "They mutilated him. It was during the Battle of the Milky Mountain when I was just a child. I wasn't even supposed to be there, but there had been peace at the fort for so long. We thought it was safe to visit."

"You saw him die?"

"I hid and watched it all. We didn't stand a chance. The battle was over as soon as it began, but the elves stretched it out for hours, slowly torturing and killing everyone they saw."

Ramona pressed her lips together tightly. "I remember hearing about that battle. The soldiers were angry because human mercenaries had just destroyed a small elven village whose men were all away fighting the war. They wanted revenge."

Isa stiffened again. "My father had nothing to do with that slaughter. No one at the fort did."

"I know. I'm not saying they were right to do what they did. They weren't. Their actions were completely inexcusable." She sighed. "I'm just trying to explain why they acted as they did. War is devastating to all, and nobody ever fully escapes the devastation. Even the innocent suffer. There is never a winner, no matter who walks away victorious."

Isa sniffed again, and Ramona handed her a handkerchief. She gave her back another pat and walked over to the table. Isa sat up and wiped her face, sighing heavily. "I've had nightmares for years. They've only recently gone away. The doctor had to give me something to drink to help me sleep. She let out a humorless laugh.

"I had taken some the night that Thallan kidnapped me, actually."

"That's why you slept so soundly," Ramona said with a chuckle, trying to lighten the mood. "We wondered. That didn't seem normal, even for a human."

The woman poured her a drink and held it out invitingly. "Why don't you eat something," she said. "I know you must be hungry, even though you did eat enough for an army when you returned last night."

Isa shook her head. "I can't eat. Not right now." Powerful emotions swirled through her.

Pain at the memory of her father.

Despair at her failure.

Anger toward the assassin who had defeated her.

Guilt at making a deal with the elf and staying at his house, eating his food, and feeling what she had felt in his arms when he held her under the waterfall.

She shook her head to clear it of the unwanted memories.

Ramona ignored her protestations and brought the drink and plate of food to her, placing the glass on the nightstand and the food on the bed. When Isa didn't respond, she slid the plate closer with an encouraging grunt. Isa finally accepted it and began picking at it slowly.

"Tell me about that day," Ramona urged.

Isa hesitated. She didn't like talking about it, but the elf's concern seemed sincere. There was no judgment in her eyes nor pity—just sorrow and sympathy. Isa had never been able to talk about it before, but she wanted to now, partly because the memories had resurfaced so strongly and partly to share with Ramona how horrendous the men of her race could be.

She opened up and all the terrible things she had seen spilled out of her like a flood. Talking about it, especially with an elf, was difficult, but female elves didn't evoke the same rush of emotions as male elves. It was elven men who had killed her father. She had nothing against the race as a whole, but terror and rage overwhelmed her whenever she thought of the power and brutality of their warriors.

As Isa completed her story, Ramona shifted the discussion to other topics. She kept up a quiet, subdued conversation while Isa finished eating, understanding that her current mood couldn't handle any exuberance, and Isa was grateful.

Mainly, they discussed her new wardrobe and what she could do to stave off the boredom that came with being locked in a small chamber, alone most of the time. As they discussed these other topics, Isa's memories slowly receded to the back of her mind. They didn't vanish that day. They were still there, a dull ache that never quite faded away, but they were no longer at the forefront.

She could keep them locked up for now, at least, as long as she had the elf girl's soothing company. Ramona seemed to sense this. She stayed with her the rest of the day, only leaving briefly to grab another tray and fix the men something simple to eat. When the fire in the fireplace burned low, Ramona got up from her chair to leave.

"Goodnight, Isabella," she said.

"Isa."

"What?"

"My friends call me Isa."

A smile spread across the elf's face. "Goodnight, Isa."

"Goodnight, Ramona."

Isa sat there long after her new friend had gone, staring into the glowing embers. She knew she wouldn't sleep. She couldn't. The memories rose again in Ramona's absence, and her emotions felt raw.

She knew images of the past would torment her as soon as she closed her eyes. She snuggled into her chair, pulling her blanket up around her, and prepared to spend the night watching the fire dance.

She froze when she heard the soft click of her door unlocking. Did Ramona forget something? She hoped so. It opened quietly, and then there was silence. She waited, listening, her ears strained against the stillness. The crackling of the fire was the only sound she heard. Had she been mistaken? She turned to glance at the door and almost jumped out of her skin when she saw a man standing right beside her chair.

Her eyes shot to Thallan's face, and fury replaced surprise. All the anger, all the grief, all the pain that she had been feeling that day rose to the surface and erupted out of her like lava. It was all his fault. He tried to kill her. He had hunted her down. He had chased her into the clutches of those vile men. He had caused her to almost drown. He had made her betray her father's memory by having scandalous feelings for him.

She kicked out at him viciously.

He was an elven warrior. He was like those who had murdered her father. He was an assassin. He was her captor. He was the enemy.

She rose to her knees in her chair and began hitting him in the chest with all her strength. She put all the force she could muster into those blows. Everything she had. Tears streamed down her cheeks and sobs escaped her lips as she continued to beat on him relentlessly.

He didn't resist. He didn't try to stop her. He just stood there and took it. At that moment, all she wanted was to release the rage that had been simmering inside her ever since she was a child.

At that moment, he represented everything she hated, everything she feared. She hit him until her hands began to bleed from cuts made in her soft flesh by the braces crisscrossing his chest. He waited patiently through it all, silently. She would have noticed the strange look on his face if she had glanced up, but her eyes never left her target. So, she didn't see.

When she had finally released all her pent-up emotion and sagged back into the chair, depleted and empty, he bent over and gently picked her up. She didn't respond as he carried her to the bed and laid her on the covers. She rolled over, turned her back to him, and closed her eyes. Hoping he would go away but lacking the energy or willpower to do anything about it if he didn't, she simply ignored him. Thallan continued to sit there, his weight working like gravity, pulling her toward him.

After a few moments, Isa heard a soft, deep, melodious voice. She couldn't understand any of the words, but the tune was mesmerizing and captivating. She almost had to strain to hear it, so quietly did Thallan sing, as if he wasn't sure he wanted to share his song. The melody seeped into her in spite of herself, comforting her soul and stilling her mind. The sleep she had despaired of finally came, and she drifted off into peaceful slumber.

Chapter 4

Thallan closed and locked the door behind him. He stood and stared at it for a second before making his way down to the kitchen. Ramona sat at the table, shelling peas for tomorrow's lunch, while Balin watched her by the fire. They both turned to him when Thallan entered. Balin raised a questioning brow.

"Well?"

"You were right, Ramona. She has a great deal of pent-up anger, but I think she may have freed herself from much of it tonight."

Ramona gazed at him in confusion before realization dawned on her face.

"She attacked you!" Laughter bubbled out of her, and she had to wipe a tear away. Balin turned to Thallan in surprise.

"The human female attacked you?" he asked incredulously.

Thallan just shrugged and sat down at the table. He pulled the bread plate over and began nibbling on a slice left from dinner.

Balin glowered at his friend. "Well, I hope she didn't hurt you too badly."

The elven warrior scoffed. "No, but she did injure herself." He turned to Ramona. "You may want to go up and bandage her hands a little later. Wait until she falls into a deeper slumber, though. I'm not sure she could go back to sleep again tonight if she woke up."

Ramona glanced up and nodded.

"Why should you care?" Balin scoffed. He pulled out his dagger and began sharpening it. "She's only a human."

Thallan didn't answer, so the other man stopped what he was doing and watched him.

"I don't know," Thallan finally admitted. "I don't care. Not really. She could die tonight, and it wouldn't bother me. Not much. But I don't know... Her grief and pain. It was so intense, so raw. And it felt somewhat—familiar—somehow. I wanted to help her expel it. That's all."

He poured himself a drink and stared down into the swirling liquid. *Would* he care if she died that night? It would solve several problems—her desire for his capture, his desire for her. No. He wouldn't accept that one. True, he had felt a stirring of desire there by the waterfall, but that could be attributed to many things, primarily her lack of proper clothing and the close proximity forced on them by the narrow ledge.

He turned his goblet up and spilled its contents down his throat. "I'm going out."

As soon as he had moved out of sight, a smile split Ramona's face from cheek to cheek.

"What's got you so happy, woman?" asked Balin.

"He's starting to care about her. Don't you see? She could be the one to break the curse."

Balin snorted. "She's a human."

"And humans are the enemy. The curse said that since he shed so much of his enemy's blood on the battlefield, he would suffer from an eternal, irresistible compulsion to kill until he could learn to love an enemy and gain love from her in return. If he can love her, and she can love him, it would break the curse."

"Ugh, but she's a human. Who could love a human?" he said with disgust.

"Don't be so mean. What's wrong with her? She's actually quite pretty for a human."

"What's wrong with her? Humans are all the same—weak, helpless, little creatures that constantly lie and steal. They're never satisfied with what they have, yet they always act like they're the most important beings in the world and everyone else should bow down to their every desire."

Ramona scoffed. "You've read too many of the fairytales in *Stories from Penningdon*. Humans are not all like that. However, I do agree with you that some of the things the "heroes" in those stories do are a little disconcerting. I shudder to think that the author of that book considered some of those actions heroic. But, again, not all humans are that way. Isa is rather nice. You should spend some time talking to her and getting to know her."

"Talk to her! Woman, she's a human. What could we possibly have to talk about?"

"You're right. That's not a good idea. I wouldn't want her to get the impression that all elves are like you."

Balin glared at his mate before going back to sharpening his knife with a vengeance.

Thallan stood at the entrance to the alley. His back pressed up against the stone wall of the building behind him. Rain poured down around him, soaking everything in sight—everything except him. An old beggar walked down the road, glancing around nervously. When his eyes wandered in Thallan's direction, they shot open, and the man hurried away.

Thallan had grown so accustomed over the years to controlling the rain with his magic that he did it without thinking. But he needed to pay attention tonight. His target would be exiting the building across the street at any moment, and he shouldn't do anything to draw attention to himself.

Glancing up at how the rain obviously parted around him just overhead, he realized his mistake and released it. He grimaced when the cold drops pelted down his face. Bowing his head, he lowered his hood and scowled out at the street. He had an affinity for water, but that didn't mean he liked the feel of it soaking through his shirt on a cold, windy night.

Loud noises issued from the bar, and sour smells wafted up from vile puddles scattered around it. One man sat slumped against its wall. He bent over and spilled the contents of his stomach, only to fall over into the mess a moment later.

Humans were disgusting.

A vision of the girl rose before his eyes, and he had to stop the progression of his thoughts and correct the error in his suppositions. Not all humans were disgusting. His human would never act that way.

His human.

When had he started to think of her as his?

The banging of the door across the street drew his attention back to his task. His target stumbled out onto the road and staggered down the street. Thallan groaned. He didn't kill for the fun of it. He killed because he had to, but killing people like this...

The man deserved it. He was sure of that. But his complete helplessness right now almost made Thallan feel like he was murdering a child. If only more of his targets could be warriors or at least strong, able men who would fight back. Perhaps the act would be a little more palatable then.

With a sigh, Thallan pushed himself away from the wall and stalked after his prey.

When Isa woke the following day, her hands felt thick and awkward. She pulled them from beneath the covers and stared at the bandages wrapped around them. Then, all the memories of the previous night flooded back. A blush heated her cheeks as she remembered how she had attacked Thallan.

What must he think of her? The crazy human. The wild, out-of-control woman who was stupid enough to believe she could injure an elven warrior with nothing more than her fists.

She glared down at her bandaged hands. She felt sure she was the only one injured in that onslaught. She hoped that he hadn't been the one to bandage her hands. That would be mortifying, not to mention weird. A deadly elf assassin tending to a lowly human's hands—one who had been his target nonetheless. She laughed mirthlessly at the thought.

Isa rolled out of bed and moved to a seat near the fireplace. She sat there staring into the all too familiar flames. They seemed to mock her as they danced around freely, lunging, laughing, enjoying life as they were meant to while she sat there a prisoner of a dangerous, dark assassin. And of a hastily made promise.

She pushed herself out of the chair and wandered over to the window. Peering out into the cold darkness of the wooded landscape, she felt a chill run down her spine. Even in the unlikely event that she could escape, she still had no idea where she was. And even if she managed to find her way home, what waited for her there? Another assassin? One who wouldn't be as "generous" as Thallan?

What would Thallan do to her? Would he leave her alone if she didn't report him? His only concern appeared to be with Ramona's safety. Would he let her go if she did nothing to put that at risk? Would it matter? If her enemy still wanted her dead, what choice did she have?

Isa groaned. As much as it pained her to think it, the elf might be right. Perhaps it would be best if she waited out the month there, in the safety of his home.

Her face fell into her hands as waves of despair washed over her. What was to become of her? Where could she go when she left? And would she really be allowed to leave? Thallan had said he would release her in thirty days, but could she trust him?

The memory of a dream flickered through her mind, of Thallan singing her to sleep. It had seemed so vivid, so real. She shook her head with amusement. What were the chances of the terrible, deadly elf assassin doing something like that? Probably about the same as those of him bandaging her hands.

A light knock on the door distracted her from her musings, and to a small degree, the smell of breakfast on Ramona's tray chased away some of the clouds dampening her spirit. At least she had good food and good company in her prison, whenever Ramona had time to spare between her other duties, that is.

The elf made the bed and tidied the room while Isa ate, chatting amicably the whole time. She helped her dress and brushed through her long tresses, but she didn't bother arranging her hair or pulling it up. What would be the point? She couldn't go anywhere.

"Am I allowed to leave this room?"

"No. I'm sorry," Ramona replied reluctantly.

Isa sighed. "Why not? It's not like I'm going to try to run away. I made a promise."

Ramona continued brushing her hair, her lips pressed together tightly.

"It's just so boring being in here alone all day. Didn't you say that there was a library?"

Ramona nodded eagerly, excited at an option to help her young friend without disobeying her lord.

"I can bring you some books if you'd like."

Isa smiled sadly at her through the mirror. "I would like something to read, but—I'd much rather go to the library myself. It's hard to tell you what books I want without seeing the available choices. Besides, I feel like I'll go crazy if I have to keep staring at these walls much longer."

Ramona placed the brush on the vanity, and Isa glanced at her. She could tell by the look in her eyes that her resolve was weakening. Hope burst within the girl.

"Please. I promise I won't try to escape. I'll stay in the library or in here at all times. Well, except when I'm walking back and forth between the two." An idea caused Isa's eyes to widen. "Unless you have some elf magic that can instantly transport me between the two rooms."

Ramona chuckled. "No, we have nothing like that. At least, I don't,"

Interesting. She needed to remember to ask more about that later but for now... "Please, Ramona."

"He will be very angry."

Isa smiled at the use of the words "will be." Yes, her resolve was definitely weakening.

"Maybe he won't know. It's not like he's around much, is he? I won't tell him if you don't."

"Oh, he'll know. He knows everything that goes on around here." She sighed. "But I can handle his anger. I've done it before."

Isa felt a twinge of guilt. "I don't want to get you in trouble," she said regretfully.

"Don't worry about it," Ramona reassured her. He needs me, and he knows it. He won't do any more than growl and scowl at me. Come on, then. Did you want to go now?"

"Yes, please," exclaimed Isa with a squeal. She jumped up from her chair and followed Ramona out of the room.

The enormous double doors had Isa gawking. They projected an air of grandeur rarely seen outside of castles. Elaborate carvings adorned their surface. Twisting vines, mythical creatures, and ornate patterns seemed to come alive in the sunlight, inviting her to explore the tales and secrets hidden within the magnificent library.

With a deep breath, she pushed one of the doors open, and an echoing creak filled the air. The inside of the library was just as stunning. The towering ceilings and arched windows bathed the room in a soft, golden glow. Shelves bearing rows upon rows of books stretched across the large room, promising hours— months—years of entertainment and study. Isa breathed in the scent of old parchment. This was by far the best library she had stepped foot in, exceeding even the one in Princess Nixa's castle. With access to a room like this, she might actually enjoy staying here.

Thallan stormed down the hall. Isa wasn't in her rooms, and Ramona was suspiciously nowhere to be found either. Anger radiated off him in waves. Where had that insufferable human gone? Had she broken her promise so soon?

Had she left him after all the compromises he had made on her behalf?

He stopped and forced himself to focus past his rage. He reached his elven senses out into the atmosphere, stretching them to cover the entire mansion. Closing his eyes, the better to focus, he felt for patches of water—large patches of water—large enough to represent bodies.

Moisture hung in the air all around him, but larger spots were not as common. First, he located the well behind the kitchen. Then, a large area moved about quickly in the courtyard—most likely Balin going through his training exercises. Then another down in the cellars. So, that's where Ramona was hiding.

Finally, he sensed a slightly smaller collection of water in the library. That was her. Thallan thundered down the hall. Relief mingled with rage. She hadn't gone, but she had left the prison cell of her rooms. Did her brazen defiance mean she no longer feared him? Had she somehow discovered the power she was beginning to have over him?

She must have. How could she not? Three times, he'd had the opportunity to kill her—the intention to kill her—and three times, he had let her go. He'd even endured the onslaught from her in her chambers that night. Did she think that since he hadn't stopped her attack, that meant she needn't fear him any longer? She needn't obey him or even respect his wishes?

He needed to reintroduce her to the meaning of fear.

Isa jumped when the library doors slammed open. She looked so innocent curled up on a couch with a thick book on her lap. Innocent, and smaller than usual in the cavernous room with its heavy columns and high vaulted ceilings.

Pushing past the doors, Thallan marched over to the girl, his eyes blazing with a fury that could incinerate a mountain. "What do you think you're doing?" he growled, snatching the book from her lap.

Isa leaned away from him, startled by his violent reaction. "I was just reading."

The touch of defiance in her slightly shaky voice did nothing to cool his temper.

"You were just disobeying me," Thallan spat back, slamming the book shut and tossing it aside. "I told you to stay in your room."

"Actually, I don't think you did," Isa replied calmly. A wave of rising anger reddened her cheeks, and a spark of courage she probably shouldn't have felt in the situation shone from her eyes. "You locked my door, but I don't remember you ever telling me I couldn't leave." She raised her chin stubbornly.

Thallan's expression twisted with anger. He bent down over her, his face only inches from hers. "Just because I haven't killed you yet, don't make the mistake of thinking I won't do so." His voice, low and menacing, sent adrenaline rushing through her.

Isa gulped. "I just want to be allowed some freedom. That's not unreasonable, is it? After all, I'm not a prisoner, am I? Or am I?"

Thallan glared at her but didn't comment.

"I'm not stupid," Isa continued in a quiet voice. "I understand the terms of our deal. I won't leave, but can't I at least move around inside the house freely? It's so horrible being trapped in that room all the time," she pleaded.

Thallan narrowed his eyes. Frustration at the situation slowly replaced the overwhelming rage that had consumed him. What had he been thinking, bringing this irritating human here? He should have just completed the contract that night and saved himself this annoyance.

"If you leave these grounds, I will hunt you down and make you wish I had killed you in your sleep. Whether you go to the king's guard or not."

The threat should have terrorized Isa, but it didn't appear to have the desired effect. Instead, she looked slightly thrilled. A smile spread across her face, but she quickly subdued it. However, she didn't completely suppress the joy that bubbled out with her words.

"Yes, of course," she said with a solemn nod. "No leaving the grounds without horrible torture and death. Got it."

Thallan growled at her, cursing himself for his weakness where she was concerned. He had *never* had so much trouble assassinating someone before. Why couldn't he kill her? What was wrong with him? Without another word, he turned and left the room. He had another job to do. He didn't have any more time to waste on that annoying creature.

Chapter 5

Thallan crept through the night, following the garden wall of the Wilmen estate with silent, cautious steps. The throbbing in his head and the drive to kill had grown progressively more insistent as he traveled closer to town, almost as if the curse understood what he was going to do and was egging him on.

The night was dark and still, the only sound the distant hoot of a solitary owl. He moved slowly and steadily, careful of every step he took, his elven training ensuring he went unheard.

Stopping at the wall, he measured it with his eyes. It was high and formidable, made of thick stone bricks, with no openings or crevices to be seen. Thallan sighed; he'd have to scale it.

He ran his fingers along the wall's stones, searching for even the smallest of handholds. He wouldn't need much. Finding a tiny aperture, he gripped it with the tips of his fingers and pulled himself up. Repeating the action a few times, he maneuvered over the top, dropping lightly to the ground on the other side. He paused for a moment, allowing his eyes to adjust to the increased darkness caused by the shadows surrounding a plethora of fruit trees.

102

Thallan stayed in the shadows, using the darkness to cover his movements. Guards patrolled this area, and he found himself growing weary of the excessive slaughter often necessitated by their presence. The curse didn't require so much bloodshed. Though, Thallen guessed that wouldn't be true for much longer. For now, if he could avoid unnecessary deaths, he would.

Rounding a corner, he saw a window lit up with a soft yellow glow, its curtains fluttering in the wind. He crept closer and paused, listening for any signs of movement coming from within. All was silent.

From the light glow of the candle, Thallan could see a man working at a desk in a corner. From his position, he couldn't make out the face of the figure, but he knew it was most likely his target based on the extravagant luxury of the space. He had found him—the Duke of Wilmen.

Thallan eased himself into the room and slowly drew one of his swords. Creeping into the shadow of a wardrobe, he paused to evaluate the situation. There seemed little doubt that the man before him was the duke, but he didn't want to assassinate him until he knew for sure. How could he find out?

Scanning the room, Thallan's eyes fell on a bellpull beside the nearby bed. He had heard of those. They didn't have them in the elven kingdom. They didn't need them with their magic, but according to what he had heard, humans used them to summon servants. If he pulled that, a servant should come, and any servant who arrived would address the man by his title.

His head pounded with the impatience of the curse. He would need to act quickly, or it would drive him to kill the man before he could discover his identity, and then he would have a difficult time knowing whether he had completed his contract.

Thallan's feet barely made a sound as he shifted his weight and inched across the floor. He pulled the rope that hung by the bed and returned to his position beside the wardrobe. Now, he could only wait, the urge to kill growing stronger every second.

Finally, a light knock sounded on the door. At the man's command to enter, a small serving girl came into the room.

"You rang, Your Grace."

Thallan held his breath, listening to the man's response.

"No, I did not ring." The duke's voice was low and gruff, with an underlying note of irritation.

Thallan relaxed slightly. This was him.

As soon as the confused girl left, Thallan stepped out of the shadows. He cleared his throat to get the man's attention. His warrior's code didn't allow him to stab someone in the back when he was doing nothing more than sitting at a desk. He should be allowed to face his death.

The duke turned and gasped, his eyes widening in fear as he saw the dark figure standing before him.

"Who are you?" The middle-aged man knocked his chair over when he jumped to his feet; his thinning hair flopped where he had combed it over.

"I am the Beast," Thallan replied, keeping his voice low. "And I have come to fulfill a contract."

The duke's eyes narrowed. "What contract?"

"The contract for your death," Thallan said coldly, brandishing his sword. The curse had grown too powerful, and he could no longer resist its pull.

The duke's face paled, and he stumbled backward, upending a vase in the process. Water spilled over the stone floor like a foreshadowing of the darker, red liquid that would soon join it. The man reached behind himself and drew a sword from beneath the heavy desk. Holding it out, steady, in front of him, the duke glared at the assassin.

Good, thought Thallan through the haze of the curse, a target who wanted to fight back. He preferred those to the ones who just cowered before him as he ended their lives. Or worse, the ones who ran.

In the end, it still wasn't much of a fight. The duke didn't possess the strength and skill he might have had in his younger days. Thallan didn't draw it out. He felt no enjoyment in killing, other than the release of the pressure from the curse. However, he felt no guilt or remorse in it either, at least not in the killing of humans.

An awareness arose in him at that thought. He couldn't condemn the girl for hating all elves when he still felt the same about humans. Was he being unjust in his thoughts toward her?

Did he feel the same about humans, though? It was true that he felt no guilt in fulfilling his nightly contracts, but the men he killed were always criminals themselves. He ended their lives at the request of other criminals, but that didn't negate the fact that they, themselves, were cruel.

The girl was the only contract he had received for an innocent person. And she *was* innocent. He did not doubt that now. Regardless of how she seemed to have gotten under his skin.

Thallan cleaned his blade on the duke's bed sheets and slid it back into position. He walked through the silent phantoms floating around him and climbed out the window. Could that really be the reason why he was having so much trouble killing her—she was innocent? Was it possible that it was as simple as that after all? Perhaps his disdain was just for *corrupt* humans, not humans in general.

Even so, he was still no better than the girl. She hated him because he was an elf assassin, but she had no problem with Ramona. If she could be convinced that he wasn't evil, could she learn to overcome her negative feelings toward him someday?

Thallan pushed the thought from his mind. He must stop imagining that the human was the one who could break his curse. Yes, he admired her bravery and her kind heart. Her perseverance and her intellect. Even her stubbornness and passionate anger. And he couldn't deny that he was attracted to her physically. But she was a human—a weak, fragile, magic-less mortal. And she was so innocent of the ways of the world.

He would end up breaking her one way or another, either physically, mentally, or emotionally. At the very least, he would corrupt her. No, she couldn't be the one. He had to seal his heart tightly before she wormed her way in any further.

He would leave at the end of the month when he sent Ramona and Balin away. He'd go with them. He could find a goblin woman to break his curse. Goblins were the enemies, too, and they were strong, magic-wielding immortals like his people. He despised them just as much as he despised humans. That should satisfy the curse's requirements.

Besides, he *was* evil. The specters of the dead that encircled him attested to that. How could he convince the girl he was different than the elves who murdered her father when she saw the evidence of his kills on his clothes all the time? As long as the curse held him captive, he was a beast worthy of her hate.

So be it. If a beast he was, then a beast he would be.

Isa left the library and walked across the front hall, once again admiring the beauty of the space. The white marble tiles reflected the light of the enormous crystal chandelier. Large paintings and tapestries hung from the walls, and tall windows encased with heavy curtains let in an abundance of natural light during the day. But it was not day now. As Isa glanced around the hall, the darkness of those windows seemed to watch her as if they were living, breathing beings—sinister beings waiting only for her to turn her back.

She grabbed the smooth, polished wood of the stair railing, ready to escape to the welcome cheeriness of her bedchamber, when she heard the front door open. She gripped her books to her chest, but one slipped off the stack and fell to the ground. The thump of its landing echoed around the vast entry hall like the clanging of a bell. Her heart beat a little faster as Thallan turned toward her.

His black clothes fit snuggly on his body beneath his billowy cape. His long, silver hair was pulled back, revealing a face that was both beautiful and terrifying. It was this face that drew her attention. Blood splattered across it, stark and vivid against his pale skin. His eyes were emotionless, his expression empty.

Isa felt her mouth go dry, and her hold on the books tightened. She had seen him covered in blood before, but the vacant emptiness of his eyes—that was new. The elf assassin had returned. He stepped closer, and she could see the dark splotches on his black clothing that could only be blood—the patterns so closely resembled the lines on his face. Suddenly, she was reminded of the violence and death that had taken her father.

She stood there and stared at him.

He stood there and stared at her.

He didn't smile. There was something so menacing in his expression that even the idea of running from him terrified her. A stray thought passed through her mind, making her wonder if he would enjoy the chase.

"Why do you kill?" Isa blurted the words out, breaking the silence before her mind even realized she wanted to ask the question.

"Humans are the enemies," he replied, his voice flat. He stared into the distance.

Isa felt anger bubble up inside her. "Elves killed my father," she said, her voice shaking. "They tortured him before they ended his life. He was no threat to them. It is elves who are brutal, evil, not humans."

Thallan turned to look at her sharply. "Some humans are just as bad," he said through gritted teeth. "I kill the bad ones."

Isa scoffed, unable to comprehend the elf's twisted logic. "And who decides who's bad? You? You don't get to play judge, jury, and executioner," she snapped, her eyes flashing angrily.

Thallan's expression remained impassive, but the air around him grew colder. "I do what I have to do."

"Do you enjoy it?" she asked, her voice barely above a whisper.

He turned to face her completely, his expression unreadable. "No," he said, his voice low. "But death comes to us all eventually. Even we immortals are not totally immune to it. Sometimes, it is better for everyone else if it comes to certain people a little sooner than originally intended."

"What about me?" Isa asked, her voice shaky. "Why were you going to bring an early end to me?"

Thallan took a step closer, and Isa imagined she could see a black fog surrounding him like an aura of evil. She closed her eyes, trying to calm herself.

"Any woman who uses her beauty to entrap men, to con them out of their money, to rip them from the trusting arms of their families, doesn't deserve to continue breathing."

Isa's eyes shot open. "What!"

"Do you deny it?" he asked. His deep blue eyes seemed to bore into her soul.

"Yes! Of course, I deny it. Who told you that?" she asked, outraged.

The sudden fierceness of her anger and surprise lent credence to her words and reaffirmed the conclusion he had already reached.

"It's a good thing that I didn't kill you then, isn't it."

"Yes," she pushed the words out through clenched teeth. "Who told you that?" she repeated insistently.

He shrugged. "It was written into the contract."

Isa's face lit up with sudden understanding. "Princess Nixa."

Yes, those words seemed to confirm it. That certainly sounded like something the spoiled princess would say. Isa shuffled her books to one hand and rested the other on her hip.

"She's always hated me, but when Lord Alistair began to show special interest in me, I knew she wouldn't stand by idly for long. I just had no idea she'd go to such extremes."

"It is possible." Thallan bent down and picked up the book she had dropped, returning it to the top of her stack. Then he turned to go.

"Wait," Isa held out a hand to stop him. "Why?"

He stared at her questioningly, not understanding.

"Why did you let me live?"

The man's lips twisted in a sneer. "Why would I tell you that?"

110

"Please. I want to know."

The assassin's eyes flickered to hers, and for a moment, she thought she saw something softening in his gaze. He hesitated, clearly not wanting to answer.

"Please."

He frowned. "Lying there in the moonlight that night, you looked guiltless, pure. I know that appearances can be deceiving, but I also recognized you, of course, from when you helped me. Regardless of what the letter said, I began to doubt. Contrary to what you may believe, I don't kill indiscriminately. I attempt to avoid harming those who are innocent. Unless they try to prevent me from performing my duties, that is." Thallan watched her reaction closely. "So, I brought you back here. If you turned out to be what the letter claimed, I could always kill you later."

"And have I?" she asked. "Do you believe the letter now?"

Thallan regarded her carefully for a moment. "No, I don't believe you are like that. A pest? Yes. An annoying inconvenience? Definitely. But an enslaver of men? No. At least, not intentionally so." He turned to go.

She didn't know what she wanted to say, but she wasn't ready for him to leave yet.

"Thallan."

He gazed at her curiously.

"Thank you for not killing me. And for letting me hide out here. And for rescuing me from those horrible men. I know you hate humans and see me as a nuisance, so I appreciate the patience you have to endure my presence." She tucked a stray strand of hair behind her ear. "I'll try not to be so argumentative and annoying all the time."

He snorted, and she thought she saw a tiny smile tug at the corner of his lips just before he turned his back to her and headed down the unlit hall. "That would be appreciated," he said as he disappeared into the darkness.

Princess Nixa stared out the castle window and watched the pale moonlight sparkle on the lake. The night sky was clear, and the stars twinkled merrily, but the peacefulness of the scene didn't penetrate the roiling turmoil that filled her heart. She had hired an assassin to murder someone. It didn't seem quite real.

It wasn't as if she had intentionally searched for a killer. It had occurred almost accidentally. She'd originally just planned on spreading malicious gossip about Isabella to ruin her reputation. The stranger had just happened to be nearby when she complained to her friends. The royal "problem-fixer" he had called himself. He could take care of this for her if she'd like.

What had she done? Nixa bit her lip and began pacing her room. She hadn't known the man was going to contact an assassin. "Take care of this" could mean a variety of things.

This wasn't her fault. He didn't tell her he meant to have the pest killed until the night before it was scheduled to happen. What could she have done about it then? It wasn't as if she could warn the girl. *By the way, Isabella, I wanted to let you know that I've accidentally hired an assassin to kill you. Good luck with that.*

Yeah. That would have gone over well. She couldn't have told the man to cancel it either. How would that have made her look? Like a child who couldn't handle the harshness of the real world. That's how it would have made her look.

She was a princess, and she would be queen someday. She had to show her subjects that she had what it took to do whatever needed to be done. That included being ruthless when the occasion called for it.

What to do now, that was the question. Isabella was gone, but they hadn't found a body. Was she dead or not? If she still lived, did she know what Nixa had done? Would she tell anyone?

She'd kill that royal "fixer" if she ever saw him again. He hadn't fixed anything. He'd only made things worse. If Isabella came back and told anyone... Well, Nixa would be the one in trouble then.

She needed to come up with some explanation as to why the lady had suddenly disappeared without a trace—and fast! It wouldn't take long before rumors began circulating that something sinister had happened. She would have to get her rumors out there first. She would write a letter.

Nixa hurried over to her desk and pulled out some paper. Tapping her quill pen against her chin, she thought. It would be best if the letter appeared to come from Isabella. She had seen enough of her handwriting that she felt confident she could imitate it passably well.

It should be a confession letter. That thought brought a big smile to Nixa's face. She'd have the lady confess to a whole list of crimes against men—just like the fixer said he had put in the assassin's letter. Then, she'd say that she had run away with a traveling merchant to escape the consequences of her actions. That might be believable if she included that some of the men she'd hurt were beginning to get angry at her for leaving them.

Ruining Isabella's reputation was what Nixa had intended initially, after all. This way, if it turned out she still lived, at least she wouldn't be welcomed back or believed. After much thought and meticulous wording, Nixa completed the letter. She pulled the bell, summoning a servant, and sent him after Lady Willamina, the biggest gossip in her circle of friends. Nixa often made use of her eager gullibility. It would prove especially beneficial tonight.

Princess Nixa chose her words carefully. "Lady Willamina, do you know who left this letter on my desk?" she asked innocently. "You were here when we met before tea. Did you see anyone drop it?"

"No, Princess."

Nixa tapped the folded paper against her lip. "How odd. Who could have left it?" She flipped it over and stared at the wax seal. No imprint indicated the sender's identity, an intentional move on her part.

Lady Willamina excitedly entered into the mystery.

"Surely," Nixa continued conspiratorially, "we would have known if one of our ladies dropped it. They are with us all the time."

"Right," agreed Willamina, clearly not following where Nixa was going.

"So," Nixa prompted, "someone else must have left it when we were gone."

Willamina's eyes lit up with understanding. "They must have snuck in here, but who could it have been."

Nixa made a show of turning the letter over and examining it carefully. "It was on the bottom of a stack of papers, so it could have been here for days. Hmm, has anything happened in the last few days that might have led to someone leaving a secret letter in here?"

Willamina stared back at her blankly. And Nixa had to swallow a groan of frustration. Maybe she should have called in someone smarter.

"Let's open it," she suggested, deciding that hints were getting nowhere.

"Yes, yes," the lady responded eagerly.

Nixa took her time, getting her letter opener and dramatically sliding it under the seal. She unfolded the letter and glanced at it briefly before thrusting it out at her friend. "You read it. I'm too nervous," she said.

Lady Willamina grabbed the letter and eagerly began reading, her voice rising higher and higher as she progressed through the titillating confession contained in its lines. When she finished, she stared at the princess with a mix of horror and pleasure on her face. Nixa pasted an appropriate expression of shock on hers.

"Oh, my!" she said. "We probably shouldn't tell anyone about this," she added quietly.

Willamina looked surprised and a bit disappointed.

"After all," continued Nixa, "it would ruin her reputation."

"Oh, yes, definitely."

Nixa glanced at the letter. "Would you mind getting rid of that for me?" she asked.

Willamina clutched the paper to her chest protectively. "Oh, yes, of course, Your Highness."

"Well, it's getting late, Willamina. I think I'm going to turn in. I'll see you tomorrow."

With frantic, clumsy curtsies, Willamina rushed out of the room.

Nixa smiled as the door shut behind her. She had no doubt the news would spread to the whole kingdom by morning.

Chapter 6

Isa sat by the fire in the dimly lit confines of her room, chewing on the corner of her lip. She couldn't pull her eyes away from the letter. Balin had found it posted on a board in the middle of the merchant's district in town. This— this malicious lie, hung up for all to see. Even worse, he had said that the man told him it was one of many copies made and distributed throughout the kingdom.

In a daze, she left her room, her fists clenched so tightly that her nails cut into her skin. After passing through the halls in a blind stupor, she finally found herself in the overgrown garden. Looking around, she spotted an old concrete bench and sat down, staring across the tangle of vines, weeds, and scattered flowers, seeing none of it.

Her thoughts raced around in her head. Her heart pounded so hard she feared it would burst out of her chest. She would never be able to recover from this. She had to get away from there. From the entire kingdom.

But where could she go? She had nowhere to run to, no one to turn to. She was all alone.

The letter had accused her of being a gold digger, a manipulator, and a seductress. It claimed that she had used her beauty to deceive Lord Alistair, along with many other men. And worst of all, it said she had run away because she knew she was guilty.

None of it was true. Isa had tried to be kind to Lord Alistair, but that was all. She'd certainly never used her beauty to deceive anyone. The accusations were baseless, yet somehow, they had managed to shake her.

Suddenly, a hand grasped her arm, and she gasped. Her eyes shot up to see Thallan looking down at her.

"What's wrong?" he asked.

Isa hesitated for a moment at the almost friendly inquiry before finally showing him the letter. Thallan read it quickly, his face showing no emotion.

"I see," he said finally.

Isa watched him expectantly, hoping for some reassurance or explanation, perhaps some advice. But Thallan simply handed the letter back to her and turned to leave.

"Wait!" Isa called after him. "What am I supposed to do? Where can I go? I can't stay in this kingdom. Balin said this letter has been distributed everywhere. The accusations in it are ridiculous, but people will believe them. I'll be branded a harlot of the worst sort."

Thallan frowned. "This changes nothing. You were always going to have to leave."

Isa clenched her teeth. "That's it? Don't you have any advice you can offer? It is partially your fault that I'm in this situation after all."

Thallan raised an eyebrow. "Would you prefer that I had killed you? I could remedy that mistake now if you'd like," he said, his hand moving toward his dagger.

"No, of course not," Isa replied, her frustration deflating. "I just don't know what to do. I could use some help coming up with a plan."

Thallan shrugged. "Leave the kingdom. Go somewhere where no one knows you. Start a new life."

"I can't just leave," Isa said. "I have nothing. No money, no resources."

"Did you have any money in your old rooms?" he suggested. "Anything you could sell? What did you live off of before?"

"I have my jewels in my bedroom and my purse. That would help for a little while. I received a regular income from the bank, but what if Princess Nixa has someone watching my account? They'll know I'm alive if I try to collect that."

Thallan studied her. "I can get what you need from your rooms. I assume they wouldn't have touched anything yet since they can't prove you're dead."

"Probably not."

"I'll go tonight after I've taken care of my other business."

Isa flinched at that inference.

"What do you need me to get, and where is it?" he asked her.

Isa sighed. "I have a small purse and stash of jewels hidden in a false compartment in my vanity. They should be enough to sustain me for a while."

Thallan nodded. "I'll retrieve them for you."

"Thank you. I appreciate your help."

Thallan nodded before disappearing into the shadows.

Isa watched him go. He was indeed a strange assassin—a strange man. At times, he frightened her to her very core, but at other times, he evoked quite different emotions. She leaned back against the stone wall behind her. He wasn't what she had thought an elven warrior would be like. Well, he was, but he wasn't.

He was just as cold and deadly as she would have expected. She closed her eyes and brought to mind the image of him bursting from the shadowy trees and slaughtering the men who were attacking her. Cold and deadly could be good at times. She had certainly appreciated those qualities in him then.

That image morphed into another one. No, not an image exactly, more of a feeling. The feeling of his arms wrapped around her. Of his strong, muscular chest pressed up against her cheek. Of the sound of his heartbeat. Of his hand brushing her hair aside. He could be gentle, too, even when bringing death.

A blush heated her face at the memory. She had almost lost her hatred of his kind while standing there in his warm embrace. Even when he was poised to kill her, she could feel something more from him, and it awakened a response in her. What was it?

Kindness? Perhaps.

Affection? Maybe.

Attraction? Possibly.

She was undeniably attracted to him. Too attracted to him. He *was* an elf, and while they were enemies, no one could deny their physical appeal. But elven women were stunning—Ramona was proof of that—and even though Isa was considered beautiful by human standards, she surely couldn't appeal to an elven man.

Why hadn't he killed her then? Why had he offered her a compromise instead? It would have made more sense to just dispose of her. The elves who had killed her father would have. Could he be different?

How could he be? He was an assassin. He murdered humans every night. How could he justify that? He claimed to only kill bad people, but how could he know for sure? He'd almost killed her.

But he hadn't, a small voice reminded her. And he hadn't killed her by the river, nor by the waterfall. He didn't stop her when she beat on him in her chambers, either. Why not? He had repaid the debt he owed her that night when he'd let her live and brought her here. He didn't owe her anything else. He had undoubtedly *intended* to kill her. Why hadn't he?

Isa absentmindedly picked a wildflower growing by her bench and twirled it in her fingers. Was it possible? No, that was ridiculous. If Thallan had been human, she wouldn't have had any question about it. Human men had always thrown themselves at her feet, but Thallan was an elf. Elves hated humans. He couldn't be attracted to her. He certainly couldn't have any affection for her. Kindness, maybe. Pity, perhaps. But that was all it could be.

He had been surprisingly gentle with her, though. Even when he was about to kill her at the waterfall, he had been incredibly tender about it. Even in the library, when he had threatened to hunt her down and torture her if she left, there had been something there—something she couldn't quite describe that made her feel that he would never actually follow through with it.

Maybe he wasn't quite as evil as she had first thought. Maybe he did only kill bad people. Would that make it better? Would that make it okay?

Ugh! Isa pushed herself to her feet. She was thinking too much about the man. She wadded up the letter she still clutched in her hand. She would stay here the rest of the month, and then she'd leave him behind. In the meantime, she'd banish him from her thoughts. She had other things to think about. How hard could it be?

Isa's life fell into a pattern over the following days. Thallan had retrieved the items from her rooms in the castle, and she began considering where she could go and what she could do once she got there. There was always the option of marrying, but she didn't want to do that, not out of necessity.

She spent the majority of her time in the library reading up on the different kingdoms. However, after encountering a blood-soaked Thallan in the hallway so late that one night, she had begun going to the library in the mornings instead of after dinner.

It wasn't that she wanted to avoid him exactly. On the contrary, she considered him a puzzle she was eager to solve. It was more that she preferred not to encounter him when he returned from a mission, covered in the evidence of his actions.

Sometimes, he came to the library when she was there. He had appeared surprised to see her the first time and had hesitated at the door as if he were considering leaving. She had been surprised as well. He hadn't struck her as an avid reader. But true to her promise, she didn't bother him. She glanced up, nodded a greeting, and returned to her book.

They had shared the room several times since then, in complete silence each time. And it was driving Isa crazy. What was he reading? What did an assassin read? *One Hundred and One Ways to Kill Someone*? He could probably write that book.

She chuckled softly to herself. Maybe he was reading a romance novel. *Let's see*, she thought, *what kind of romance novel would a deadly elf assassin read?* A romantic comedy? A story about sweet summer love? No. Any romance he read would be more likely to have the hero pushing his love interest up against the wall and holding her hands captive above her head while he kissed her passionately.

It was growing uncomfortably warm in there. Isa fanned herself with her book as she pushed the newly formed images from her mind. She jumped slightly when Thallan rose from his seat by the window and walked across the room.

She watched him as he disappeared into the stacks. She couldn't tell for sure where he went. However, the last time he'd gone to get a book, she thought she'd caught a glimpse of his dark shirt in the far corner one row over. Yes. There it was again. Up high. She'd have to check to see if there was a ladder over there when he left. Isa bowed her head over her book again and pretended to read when he walked back by.

An hour later, Thallan returned his mysterious book to its mysterious shelf and left the library. Isa jumped up immediately and hurried to that corner. As she had hoped, a ladder stood propped against the shelf.

Curses. This whole row of books dealt with curses. Why would he be reading about curses?

Later that evening, Isa tried to ease into the subject when she and Ramona were eating dinner in her rooms.

"I have a question."

"What?"

"I couldn't help but notice that the outside of this manor is a complete mess. It looks like a ruin like it would fall if you blew on it, but the inside, especially the library, is perfect, absolutely beautiful. And it's filled with books. How's that possible?"

Ramona laughed. "Elf magic."

"What do you mean?"

"Thallan had my cousin transport the interior of his home here, inside this old, abandoned manor. It didn't affect the exterior of the house, but the inside is Thallan's home. You are staying in his sister's old bedroom."

"I thought you said elves didn't have transportation magic."

"I said that *I* didn't, not that no elves did. We all have some magical abilities aside from our core magic. My cousin's happens to be transportation."

Isa laughed, but as interesting as this was, they'd gotten off-topic.

"Anyway, I love the library. There are so many books on so many topics. I was surprised that Thallan spends so much time there, too."

"Oh, does he?" Ramona stood and began stacking the empty dishes back onto the tray.

"Yes. He seems particularly interested in the books about curses."

"Hmm." Ramona took a damp cloth and wiped down the table.

"Why is that, do you think?"

"I'm sure I wouldn't know." The girl wouldn't meet Isa's eyes.

"Ramona. You *do* know. You just don't want to tell me. What are you hiding?"

"I better get this tray back down to the kitchen. It's getting late. I'll say, 'good night' now."

"Ramona!" Isa called out after her, but the elf practically ran from the room.

First thing the next morning, Isa went to the library and chose a book from the 'curses' section. Quickly climbing down the ladder, she rushed over to a seat by the fireplace that afforded her a better view down that row. She snuggled into her chair and opened the book on her lap.

The tome was ancient, its pages crisp and yellow. She handled the book carefully as she settled in to read. She'd been perusing its pages for about an hour when the door opened, and Thallan entered. She watched him out of the corner of her eye as he approached his special shelf.

125

He glanced over the books, clearly noticing that one was missing. His eyes shot to her, and she looked down quickly. He pulled a book off the shelf and came to sit in the seat directly across from her. He'd never sat so close before. He'd always chosen a chair on the other side of the room.

Isa's heart rate increased, and the words of her book swam on the page, but she didn't lift her head, still pretending to read. Thallan opened the book he had brought and flipped to the middle.

"So, when did you become interested in curses?" His tone lacked its usual animosity, but a disapproving timbre filled the deep voice.

Isa attempted to sound casual as she responded. "Oh, I'm not sure. I've just always been fascinated by the subject, I suppose." She turned the page as if engrossed in its contents.

"Hmmm," he said, bending his head over his book while still keeping an eye on her. "What about the topic has you so intrigued?"

Isa glanced up at him, managing a weak smile. "I'm interested in learning about the signs of a curse," she said, deciding to try the truth.

"Ah." He glanced at the title of her book. "You should read chapter eight, then. That's where it begins to address that subject."

"Really?" she said, surprised at his helpfulness. She eagerly flipped the pages over to chapter eight. He also turned back to his book, and they read in silence until Ramona pushed a cart of food into the room.

The elf woman seemed slightly taken aback at the sight of them sitting so closely, but she didn't comment.

"Are you hungry?" she asked.

Isa looked up eagerly. "Yes, please. I'm starving." Ramona parked the cart between their two chairs and quickly left them alone. Isa closed her book and set it on the table beside her chair. Thallan didn't move, but Isa could feel his eyes on her as she reached for a cookie. She tried to ignore him, but the silence was deafening. Finally, she couldn't take it anymore.

"Thallan?" she said softly, watching as he slowly raised his head to look at her. "Are you cursed?"

He seemed taken aback by the directness of the question. "What makes you think that?"

Isa hesitated for a moment, then took a deep breath. "I saw you reading the books on curses, and Ramona wouldn't tell me anything when I asked her about it. In fact, she went out of her way to *avoid* telling me anything. That, in itself, was a bit suspicious. It wasn't difficult to figure out."

Thallan leaned forward, his eyes locked on hers. "And if I am, what do you plan to do about it? Tell the guard?"

Isa shivered involuntarily at the iciness coating his words.

"I don't plan on doing anything," she replied quickly. "I just want to understand. Maybe I can help you."

Thallan snorted in disbelief. "You? A human, help me? Don't be ridiculous."

Isa huffed in frustration. "Just because I'm human doesn't mean I'm useless. I want to help if you'll let me."

Thallan studied her for a moment, then leaned back in his chair. "Why?"

Isa shrugged, feeling a little embarrassed. "I don't know. I just—I don't like seeing you so angry all the time. And I want to help if I can. And..." She picked at a loose thread on her chair. "I don't want you to be a killer anymore like the warriors who murdered my father."

There was a long pause, and Isa held her breath, waiting for his response. Finally, Thallan let out a deep sigh and closed his eyes. When he opened them again, a mixture of pain and resignation filled them.

"Isa, I was a warrior before the curse, and I'll be a warrior after the curse. Nothing will change that."

"But you won't be an assassin anymore? You won't continue to kill humans?"

"I won't be an assassin anymore," he agreed. "I'll return to my kingdom and only kill in battle or while protecting my people."

"That's all I can ask, then. I still want to help you."

"I don't know if anyone can help me," he said softly. "I did something long ago, and now I'm paying for it. The curse is a reminder of the lives I took. It's a constant reminder of the beast that I am. That's my name, you know." He glanced over at the fire. "The name people ask for when they want me to do a job for them. The Beast."

Isa felt a pang of sympathy for him. She reached out a hand, hesitating momentarily before placing it on his arm. He didn't jerk away. He just stared at it until she slowly removed it.

"You're not a beast," she said softly. "You're a person, just like everyone else. And everyone makes mistakes."

"It wasn't a mistake."

"What?"

"What I did." He stared directly into her eyes, his light blue orbs piercing her deep green ones. "It wasn't a mistake. I meant to take the lives I took."

"Oh," her face paled.

"It was during the last goblin war. We joined the forces from Allanar. We utterly overwhelmed the goblin army, wiping out everyone who didn't run in terror."

Isa's breath grew harsher, but she didn't interrupt him. She wanted to know what had happened.

"Many of them died by my hand. At one point, I was separated from my men and surrounded by the enemy. A goblin mage was in their ranks. They fought fiercely, but they couldn't stand against me."

For a moment, Isa almost thought he was bragging, but an intensity filled his gaze, a fierceness that only bespoke the truth.

"I destroyed them all. The mage was the last to fall, and he cursed me with his dying breath."

"What did the curse say?" Isa asked.

"In shadows deep and darkness bound,
I curse thee, elf, to the battleground.
Both family and friends beware,
With enemies, this end they'll share.

Death you have brought to goblin foes,
Death you'll bring..."

Thallan suddenly stopped.
"Is that it?"

129

"So, you see," said the elf, ignoring her question. "I am cursed to feel an uncontrollable urge to kill because of all the death I dispensed on his people. He expected me to return to my kingdom and decimate them, but I came here instead."

Isa lowered her brows in confusion. "That's an odd way to end a curse. The last line doesn't rhyme. It just stops. Are you sure there's no more to it?"

Thallan growled at her. "That's all you need know."

"But isn't there some way to break it? Often, the solution to a curse is stated in the curse itself. Did it not mention anything?"

Thallan's glare once again turned icy. "If you want to help me break the curse, you must not depend on anything stated in it."

"But."

"The solution hinted at in the curse could never happen. It shouldn't happen. The consequences would be worse than the curse itself." He slammed his book shut and rose from his chair. "Good day, Isabella."

Isa watched him leave, puzzled. Surely, if the curse mentioned a solution, he would try to exploit it. Now, she was even more curious than she had been before. She grumbled to herself about pigheaded elves as she returned to her book.

The water in the tub rippled as Thallan stepped in and sat down. He watched as the clear water turned dark with dirt and blood. The newest addition to his haunting entourage hovered before him as he washed. The specter stared as if to tell the assassin that he could never be clean of the things he had done. Thallan didn't argue. He knew the phantom's eyes spoke the truth.

He brought his hands together in a double fist, and the dirty water in the tub floated in the air for a moment before it fell into the drain at the far end of the bathing room. Releasing his grip, Thallan opened his hands, and the tub filled with fresh water. He leaned back and closed his eyes.

Visions danced through his mind, refusing to give him peace. Visions of a battlefield from long ago. Blood painted the grass. Bodies lay scattered everywhere. The pungent smell of fresh death filled the air. The sky, itself, had lines of red mixed in with its blue, as though the blood of the slain had risen high up onto its canvas.

Warriors stood in groups around the field. Only Thallan stood alone, his chest rising and falling in his armor. The sword in his right hand dripped red as he bent over a short goblin cowering at his feet.

Thallan's face was twisted with rage. His piercing blue eyes, encircled by a rim of silver, held a deep loathing. Only in times of extreme emotion did that silver appear, a harbinger of things to come. It would have been a captivating sight if not for the raging animosity in his gaze. The unfortunate soul on the ground stared up into those eyes, wondering if there was any mercy in the heart of that warrior prince. He quickly decided there was not.

Dipping his hands in his own blood, the mage swiftly smeared it across the ground. His murmurs seemed to slow time as the wind carried his words through the air.

"In shadows deep and darkness bound,
I curse thee, elf, to the battleground.
Both family and friends beware,
With enemies, this end they'll share.

Death you have brought to goblin foes,
Death you'll bring 'til love like a rose
Grows in your heart for foe most fair,
And love's returned with heartfelt care.

My final breath, this curse shall weave,
Till love's embrace, your soul's reprieve.
When loved is found, pure and true,
The curse will end, and all be new."

With those words, the creature's life faded away, leaving behind only the echo of his dark incantation.

Thallan opened his eyes with a jolt of energy. He stood quickly, soaking everything nearby with the displaced water. His chest heaved as he forced himself to catch his breath. He couldn't let his guard down for even a moment without his memories haunting him. He wished he could wipe the visions of that abominable day from his mind.

Water streamed down his body as he stumbled to the edge of his bed. He grasped its wooden frame for support and leaned against it. This was the man Isa wanted to help. Kind, generous, brave, clever Isa wanted to save a monster—a beast.

He didn't regret his actions that day. They were at war. He only did what he had to do. But Isa deserved better.

The bedpost cracked in his iron grip, splinters tearing into his flesh. He pulled them out, and the wounds on his hands healed quickly as he watched with blank, empty eyes. The spirits laughed as they floated around him.

Thallan ran his hand over his face. Would destruction and death haunt him forever? Maybe that was all he deserved.

Chapter 7

A dark figure stood in the shadows of the baker's shop on Main Street. He had been there all night for the past two nights, waiting. His contact had told him that the house across the street was one of the Beast's upcoming targets. And the Beast was his. Not a kill target. He knew he didn't stand a chance against the assassin, not if there was any truth to his reputation. No, he targeted him for a different reason. Information.

The princess was in a difficult situation, and she blamed it on the intermediary who had hired the Beast for her. Lady Isabella had disappeared, but without a body, there was no way of knowing if she lived or died. If she lived, it was always possible she would return and cause trouble, even with the rumors that had been successfully spread.

The cowardly intermediary didn't dare question the Beast about it, so he'd offered the job to the Dark Blade. The man was no fool. The Beast had so many contracts because he was the best. He was no one to be trifled with. He had earned his name. However, despite the risks, the money was too much to ignore.

He would only follow him that night. Discover where he lived. See if there was any sign of the girl. Then, he could go from there.

After a while, he saw a shadow that appeared to move. It came from the house across the street and flowed down the road. The Dark Blade hesitated momentarily, unsure if what he had seen was a person or a trick of the night. Then, he saw it again, easing around a street corner. That must be him.

Staying as far back as he dared without losing his prey, the Blade followed. At times, the task seemed impossible, like following a vapor down a misty road. He often lost track of him, only to spot something farther ahead that might or might not be his quarry.

By the time he reached the city gates, he no longer knew if he was still tracking the same individual, or even if what he followed was a person at all. Outside the city, the dark mass disappeared off the side of the road into the forest. That would make sense. The Beast could hide out here away from prying eyes and still stay close by.

As soon as the shadow was swallowed by the trees, it vanished altogether. The Dark Blade stood still, listening for the sounds of the forest. Only silence met his ears. Not even the crickets chirped. Something was wrong. He felt eyes on him from all directions as if the trees themselves watched him.

The Blade's instincts kicked in, and he drew his weapon, a sleek black sword that glinted in the moonlight. He slowly made his way toward the spot where the shadow had disappeared, his senses on high alert. As he stepped deeper into the woods, he heard a faint rustling, like something small scurrying across the forest floor.

Suddenly, he felt a sharp prick in his neck and stumbled forward, dropping his sword. The world around him swam in and out of focus, and he struggled to stay conscious. Through his blurry vision, he saw a figure approaching, tall and menacing.

"Who are you?" The Dark Blade croaked out.

The figure chuckled, a sinister sound that sent shivers down the Blade's spine. "I am the Beast," he said, his voice deep and gravelly. "And you, my friend, are my prey."

The Dark Blade tried to fight off the effects of whatever drug had been injected into his neck, but his body was slowly failing him. He watched helplessly as the Beast loomed closer, his blue eyes, ringed with silver, examining him.

"You are one of the best, for a human," the Beast said, circling the Blade like a predator. "But even the best must eventually fall to a superior force."

The Dark Blade gritted his teeth, trying to summon the strength to fight back, to resist the poison, but it was no use. He could feel it seeping through his veins. He had known better and decided to take the risk anyway. He should have expected no other outcome.

"Who are you, and why are you following me?" The Beast pushed the man's chin up with the flat of his sword.

The Blade narrowed his eyes at the man standing before him. He may be at his mercy, but that didn't mean he had to satisfy his curiosity.

"I don't have a contract for you, and the bloodlust is gone, so I'd prefer not to dirty my hands anymore tonight. However, I will if you make it necessary. Who are you, and why were you following me?"

The Dark Blade took a deep breath, feeling the pull of unconsciousness threatening to take hold. But he couldn't let himself go just yet. Perhaps he could discover the information he sought by giving the Beast what he wanted. It appeared to be his only option, especially if he wanted to have any chance of surviving this encounter. It was becoming increasingly difficult to hold back the darkness, so he spoke quickly.

"I'm here for Lady Isabella."

The Beast's eyes narrowed. "What do you know about Lady Isabella?"

"Not much," the Blade admitted. "But I know you were hired to kill her."

The Beast chuckled. "I'm hired to kill a lot of people. What makes you think I was hired for her specifically?"

"The intermediary who hired you mentioned her by name," the Dark Blade said.

The Beast's expression hardened. "And what do you want with Lady Isabella?"

"A friend of mine is worried about her," the Dark Blade said, his vision blurring more thoroughly around the edges. "She's gone missing, and he thinks she might be in danger."

The Beast studied him for a long moment. "No," he said. "You're an assassin just as I am. Somebody hired you to find her and finish the job if she still lived. *That* is the truth, is it not?"

The Blade gritted his teeth, not wanting to give in to the Beast's accusations but not feeling like he had much choice. "Yes," he finally admitted.

The Beast's eyes narrowed, and the Dark Blade could feel his grip on consciousness slipping. He fought to stay awake, to keep from falling into the darkness. It was a losing battle, though. His body was too weak.

"Tell your contact that Lady Isabella is dead. I killed her myself."

"Then, where is her body?" His voice sounded weak and hollow in the silence of the night.

Thallan's stomach twisted at the words he was about to say. They stuck in his throat, but he forced them out. He had to make the man believe him, no matter what he had to say to do so. Only if they thought the girl was dead would they leave her alone. Twisting his lip in distaste, he answered.

"I took her with me. She was so lovely, I decided to have some fun with her before I dispatched her." His nose crinkled in a sneer. "Her body will never be found. And if I ever catch you following me again, I'll dump your body in the same place."

The darkness finally overtook the Blade, and he slumped to the ground unconscious.

Isa paced back and forth in her room, unable to shake off the strange conversation she'd had with Thallan about the curse. There was so much she didn't know, so much that he refused to tell her. She had always been a curious person, and this time was no different.

She sighed, knowing she couldn't sleep until she had more information. After all, she had to learn everything that was said if she wanted to have any hope of helping him break it. At least, that's what she told herself. Satisfied with that justification, she grabbed her robe and made her way to Thallan's chambers.

When she reached his door, she hesitated for a moment. She wasn't sure if disturbing him was a good idea, but her curiosity won out. She knocked softly, but there was no answer. Surely, he would be back by now. It lacked only an hour till sunrise. She tried the handle and was surprised to find the door unlocked. She pushed it open and stepped inside.

The room was relatively dark. The torches lining the hallway didn't reach far inside, so it's illumination came from the moon filtering in through the window and the soft glow of the coals in the fireplace. Isa could barely make out more than the shape of someone lying in the bed.

"What do you want, Isa?" Thallan asked.

Isa jumped at the sound of his voice. "I'm sorry for disturbing you. I couldn't sleep, and I was wondering if you could tell me more about the curse..." she trailed off, realizing how silly it sounded.

Thallan turned onto his side to face the girl, his eyes easily penetrating the darkness. He could see her quite clearly, but it was evident that her human eyes strained to see him. And here she was, alone with him in his bedroom at night. For just a moment, the words he had spoken to the assassin in the forest returned to him, and a shudder of revulsion wracked his body. He would never take a woman by force, especially one he planned to kill immediately after.

But he wondered. The curse insisted he love his enemy. Did it have to be emotional love? Would physical love work? If she were willing, that is? And he could make her willing if he wanted to. He was pretty sure about that.

The idea wasn't as repulsive to him as it would have been a week ago. He only spared a second to consider the idea. No, the goblin wouldn't have let him off that easily.

Besides, he wouldn't do anything to forge any more of a connection with her. Despite his every attempt to hold her at a distance, she continued to plague his thoughts. Something like that would only make things worse. He reluctantly pushed the idea away.

"It's late, Isa. Go to bed."

"Why won't you tell me what the rest of the curse said?"

"Because there's nothing to it. It can't help us break it, and with your determination to help me, your knowing that information might actually prevent you from being able to break the curse."

"What? How can knowing what the curse says about breaking it prevent me from breaking it? That doesn't make sense."

Thallan leaned up on his elbow, causing the sheet to slide down his bare chest. Isa's eyes had adjusted to the darkness since she'd been standing there talking to him, and a blush heated her cheeks at the sight.

"Because," he said, smirking at her obvious discomfort. He sat up further, causing the sheet to pool around his waist, completely exposing his muscled torso. He had to strangle a laugh as Isa gasped softly in response.

"Because," he said, drawing her attention back to their conversation, "if you know, you may try to force the result, and a curse cannot be broken by a forced result. It has to happen naturally."

At this point, Isa's face felt so hot that was all she could think about. Well, that was almost all she could think about. She tore her eyes away from the elf, the terrible inappropriateness of the situation finally hitting her.

"Yes, of course. You're right. I'm sorry. Good night," she stuttered. Turning quickly, she fled out the door.

Thallan laughed when she had gone. That was fun.

The stunning gown lying at the edge of the bed captured Isa's attention. She picked it up and sighed. This had to be the softest fabric she had ever touched, and she had grown up wearing the best. She held the gown against her and twirled around the room.

"Do you like it that much?" Ramona asked in amusement.

Isa gasped, then laughed lightly. "Ramona, you startled me."

Ramona walked further into the room, "My apologies. That was not my intention." She placed the box in her hands on the bed.

"What's that?" Isa asked.

Ramona gestured for her to come closer. "Open it; you'll see."

Isa spread the gown out on the bed and carefully lifted the lid of the box, her mouth making a tiny 'o' of surprise. She pulled out a pair of beautiful, sparkling silver shoes.

"What's all this for? You've already given me enough new gowns, and this one is much too fine for me to wear here where no one will see me."

Ramona huffed. "I'll see you."

Isa laughed. "Yes, but you don't care what I look like."

"And Thallan will see you," Ramona added with a wink.

"What is that supposed to mean?"

"Nothing," replied Ramona, innocently, playing with the shoes.

Isa faced her new friend with her hands on her hips. "No. Not nothing. Tell me what you mean."

"I'm tired of carrying trays all over the manor, so I've decided that both of you will at least eat dinner together in the dining room each night."

"Really?" asked Isa. She had attempted to inject a fair amount of venom in her response, but her intrigue at the idea weakened the effect. "And why, pray tell, would having dinner with Thallan warrant such a dress and shoes?"

"No reason." Ramona shrugged. "Now, let's get you changed."

"Ramona, please don't do this," said Isa as the elf helped her out of her dress.

"Do what? Help you change?"

"No. Don't put such ideas into my head."

"And why not?" The elf pulled the lovely gown tight in the back and laced it up.

142

"Because he's incredibly handsome and frighteningly appealing, but he's also an elf warrior and an assassin. And," she insisted, "he hates me as much as I hate him."

"But he's handsome, is he?"

Isa glared at the elven woman. "Oh, stop it. You know he's handsome. It'd be foolish of me to try to deny it. But that doesn't matter. There's more to a man than how he looks. And there's more to a relationship than physical attraction."

Ramona tsked and propelled Isa over to the vanity, proceeding to put up her hair.

"And in case I need to say it again, he hates me."

"Don't let that concern you. He hates a lot of people."

"Okay then, forget the fact that he hates me. Can you really see your elf warrior, that assassin, deign to have a romantic relationship with a human?"

This question made Ramona pause. "Well..."

Isa's sad smirk reflected back at her from the mirror.

"You'll just have to make him forget that."

"Forget that I'm a human?"

"Yes," Ramona mumbled through the bobby pins in her mouth.

"And just how am I supposed to make him forget that I'm a human?"

"The same way any woman has ever made a man forget something she doesn't want him to remember."

Isa blushed. "No. Please. Let's talk of something else. I can't—I can't think things like that. There could be no benefits to such thoughts, only pain."

"You never know."

"Look, even if everything you are implying takes place, even if we could forget our hatred for each other, there could be no future for us. He's immortal, and I'm not. I'll grow old and die while he stays young forever."

"Have you not heard of a blood bond?"

"What's a blood bond?"

"Never mind," said Ramona, pinning the last strand in place. "Just don't let that idea hold you back. There are ways around problems like that. There." She patted Isa's head. "You look beautiful."

"Oh, Ramona, what's the point of all this?"

Ramona stared at her in the mirror. "Isn't there anything about him that you like? Anything at all?"

"He's very attractive. As I said, I can't deny that. And I feel—strange things—when I'm around him. But..."

"Is that all, then? Surely, there's something else you like about him. Think."

"Why?" Isa whined helplessly.

"Please."

Isa let out a frustrated breath. "Well, he didn't kill me, so I suppose that's one good thing."

"And?"

Isa sighed and leaned back in her chair. "Let me see. He gave me a choice by the river when he caught up to me. He didn't just kill me; he let me choose: an easy, quick death or attempt an escape that would most likely kill me painfully. I like that he didn't force me to make what he thought was the best decision but instead, let me decide on my own, even if he thought my choice unwise."

Isa stared into the distance, reliving the past several days and examining the character of the man she thought she hated. "He rescued me from those men in the forest. He didn't have to do that, especially since he was there to kill me himself. He has a code of honor, and their actions crossed the line."

She propped her elbows on the table and rested her chin in her hands. Closing her eyes, she conjured an image of the assassin in her mind. "When he lowers his walls, there's a gentleness there—a protectiveness almost, like he would rather cherish someone than hurt them."

Isa glanced in the mirror and laughed at the smile on Ramona's face. "And he doesn't let his emotions control him," she added. "He does get grouchy sometimes, but he's quick to see reason when it's presented. There. Is that enough?"

Ramona laughed back. "It seems you've formed quite an accurate picture of him. Can you admit that he's not like the warriors who tortured and murdered your father," she asked with a sad smile.

"Yes," Isa reluctantly agreed. "I can't see him doing anything like they did."

"Then, do you have to hate him?" The elf woman asked softly, laying a hand on her shoulder.

Isa suddenly turned and stared up at her friend. "Ramona," she asked, remembering her dream. "Does Thallan sing?"

"Sing? He did at one time, but that was centuries ago. I haven't heard him sing since he was old enough to fight in his first war."

"Centuries? Exactly how old is he?"

"I believe he just turned five hundred and thirty-three."

"How old are you?" she asked curiously, hoping Ramona would overlook the rudeness of the question."

The woman bonked her on the nose. "I'm six hundred and two. Now, why did you ask about Thallan singing?"

Isa laughed. "I had a dream the other night. That day we talked about my past," she explained sheepishly.

"He came to visit me before I went to bed. When I saw him... All I could think of was the elves that had killed my father. He looked so much like them now that I knew what he was. I just reacted. And he let me."

Ramona snickered. "I heard about that."

Isa cleared her throat. "Yes, well. Anyway. After I ran out of steam, I felt empty inside. Completely exhausted. Like I couldn't care about anything anymore. Thallan picked me up and laid me on the bed. I turned my back on him and waited for him to leave, but he didn't. I must have fallen asleep then because I heard a haunting voice singing something in a different language. It was beautiful."

"That was no dream."

"How do you know?"

"Have you ever dreamed anything like that before?"

"No, but why would he do that? Why would he care if I were upset or not? I had just attacked him."

"He's not a bad man," Ramona said as she picked up Isa's discarded gown from the floor. She stared at it thoughtfully as she spoke. "Don't misunderstand. He's a fearsome warrior. He's killed innumerable foes, but he doesn't hurt the innocent, and his heart isn't stone. Before the—well, before, he was a normal elf when he wasn't fighting in a war or training for one. And even then, he was a normal warrior. I even heard him laugh on occasion. He's just different now. He's colder, harder. But I know he can change again. He can become who he once was with the right motivation." She folded the gown and laid it aside. "I just ask that you give him a chance."

"If I do, he'll break my heart," Isa sobbed.

"Maybe," Ramona agreed sadly. "But if he doesn't, your life could be much more amazing. Think about it."

Isa nodded.

"Now, come and slip on your shoes. You mustn't keep him waiting, and I must get to the kitchen. I left dinner simmering over the fire."

Chapter 8

The smell of food permeated the air. A large wooden table, polished to perfection, dominated the room, and plates laden with succulent dishes filled its length and breadth. Tall silver candle holders lined the center, and melted wax flowed down their sides like waterfalls of solidified fire.

Thallan sat at the head of the table, tapping his fingers impatiently. He couldn't understand why the woman took so long to get ready. It was just dinner. He couldn't believe Ramona had talked him into this ridiculous affair. He'd been too easy on both of them, and they'd started to take advantage of it.

He should never have let that human leave her rooms. Isa was not a guest in his house. She was nothing more than a minor inconvenience. It would be better if both women understood that.

The sound of light feet approaching made him look up, and his breath caught when his gaze landed on her. Her peach gown complimented her porcelain skin perfectly, and her long brown hair was swept up into a loose bun with tendrils falling around her face like silken spirals. She looked even lovelier than usual.

Thallan watched her approach. He stood and pulled out her seat for her when she reached the table, but he offered her no greeting. He didn't want her to think he approved of this arrangement. He picked up his knife and fork and started eating.

Isa scowled. So, he didn't want to talk. Okay, that was fine with her. She tore off a chunk of bread and took a bowl of soup.

Silence fell between them as they ate. The only sound in the room was the clicking of silverware against china. Isa tried to concentrate on her food but couldn't help occasionally stealing glances at the assassin. He was so different from anyone she had ever met before.

After her conversation with Ramona, she couldn't stop herself from noticing the strength in his broad shoulders and how his muscles rippled under his shirt. She quickly looked away, hoping he didn't see her blush. She had to distract herself.

"Why did Ramona and her husband follow you here?" she asked abruptly.

Thallan's hand froze for a split second before he continued eating. "You should ask her that," he said between bites. "And Balin is her mate, not her husband."

"What's the difference?"

"Husband and wife are human concepts. Depending on the participants and the strength of their commitments, marriages can often be weaker bonds, only existing on paper and through feeble promises. A mating bond is deeper. It comes from the sharing of blood and the binding of the essence of the two people. It is much more intimate and stronger, more permanent also than a human marriage."

Thallan considered her. He had done his research before breaking into her rooms that night. He knew men greatly desired her.

"Why have you not married?"

"Do you really want to know?"

"Why wouldn't I?"

"I don't know. I guess I'm not used to men asking questions about me. Or if they do, they do so just because they feel like politeness requires it. They never really care about the answers."

"Well, I would really like to know."

Isa opened her mouth to respond and realized she didn't know what to say. Why had she never accepted any of the men vying for her hand? Many rich, powerful, handsome men had been among her options.

"I guess I just hadn't met anyone I wanted to marry," she replied with a shrug.

Thallan could understand that. She seemed to be a very discerning woman. None of the human men would have been good enough for her. Nobody would be good enough for her.

It was becoming increasingly difficult to keep his heart protected from the human. With every encounter, it felt like she was burrowing more deeply into his soul. This couldn't happen. Even though her kindness prompted her to try to help him, she had made her hatred of his people clear.

Kindness was all it was, he reminded himself. She was kind. She had tended to his wounds that first night they met, even though anger and aversion had radiated off her like a dark aura. Nothing had changed. Why would it? He had shown her no kindness in return. Instead, he had gone out of his way to be gruff and rude to her in the hopes that she would back away. For his sake and for hers.

Even if her physical attraction to him overcame her hate, and she did allow herself to feel something for him, she would regret it in the future. Her hatred for him and his people would return in full force once the newness wore off, and that would leave them both hurt and miserable. Besides, there would be no point. The curse could only be broken by love, not lust.

He couldn't let his guard down and grow comfortable around her. And she shouldn't grow comfortable around him. He needed to keep his distance.

"Why have you never married," she asked innocently, "or have you?"

Thallan wiped his lips with his napkin and rose from his seat.

"No." He glared at her as if greatly affronted by the question. He tossed his napkin on the table and left the room. Hopefully, that would offend her enough to cause her to stay away from him.

Isa's hands clenched into tight fists as fury rose in her chest. Who did he think he was? It was just a question, one he had asked her first. She turned around when she heard the door open and saw Ramona standing there with a sorrowful expression.

"I didn't do anything," Isa said sadly.

Ramona sighed and walked into the room. "I know."

The girl's back relaxed at the response. "Why does he have to be like that?" she asked, adjusting her dress and brushing off the breadcrumbs.

Ramona sat down in the chair Thallan had vacated and smiled at Isa. "He has his reasons. He's been through a lot, and it's made him the way he is. It doesn't excuse his behavior, but it may help you to understand why he acts the way he does."

Isa leaned back in her chair and crossed her arms. "What kinds of things has he been through?"

Ramona hesitated for a moment, then decided to tell her the truth. "Thallan fought in a war a long time ago. It was a terrible conflict, and he saw things that no one should ever have to see. He lost many of his friends and comrades, and it changed him. He became more withdrawn and less trusting of others. He still carries the weight of those memories with him, and it's made him very guarded. And add to that... Well, never mind."

"Add to that what?" Isa asked, wondering if Ramona would mention the curse.

"Well, something happened, and as a result, he's had to make difficult decisions to protect his people. It's made him the way he is today. But there's still hope for him. He's not completely lost."

"I know you said that before, but do you really think so? Really?"

"I do," replied Ramona with a gentle smile. "But Thallan is not used to having people around, and he's definitely not used to people questioning him. It will take some time for him to warm up to you, but I promise you, he's not as bad as he seems. It will take patience, though. You have to be willing to give him a chance."

Isabella nodded slowly, "I'll try," she said. "But it's not going to be easy."

"I know," Ramona said, "but nothing worth having is ever easy. Just bear with him, and he might surprise you."

Isa's expression softened. She uncrossed her arms and nodded. If Ramona believed that Thallan could change, then maybe he could.

Isa went to the library after dinner. Though Thallan was usually getting ready to go out at this time, she hoped he would come by. She waited for him well into the night, but he didn't show. Disappointed, she went to bed.

"Have you noticed that Thallan seems to be staying out later on his excursions than he used to?" Ramona stood by the kitchen table, kneading dough.

"Not necessarily, but I haven't been paying that much attention," replied Balin. "Do you think the curse is getting worse?" He glanced up at her from the arrow he was making.

"I've been thinking about that. It might be."

"But why would it? If anything, shouldn't it weaken as time passes?"

Ramona rubbed her nose with the back of her hand, leaving a smudge of flour. Balin grinned but didn't say anything.

"I have a theory," she said.

"Then please share."

"I think he's beginning to have feelings for Isa."

"Ha!" Balin scoffed.

"Hear me out," Ramona insisted. "Even though she's a human, you can't deny her beauty." She raised her brows questioningly at her mate.

He frowned. "I guess she looks okay."

Ramona smiled at the concession. "And she has a wonderful personality."

"Humph."

"Which you'd realize if you spent any time with her."

"I'll just take your word for it."

"Anyway. I've noticed that he seems different around her than he was in the beginning."

Balin set down his arrow and leaned back in his chair, intrigued. "How so?"

"Well, he's more indulgent with her. He's been letting her join him in the library, and even though he's still gruff, he seems slightly more tolerant of her presence."

Balin rubbed his short beard thoughtfully.

"Interesting. But why would that make the curse worse?"

"Because if the curse feels like he's close to breaking it, his increasing attachment may be causing it to flare up."

Balin nodded, considering her theory. "It's possible. We'll have to keep an eye on things."

As if on cue, they heard the front door open. Ramona quickly wiped her hands on her apron and turned to face Thallan as he entered the kitchen.

"Good evening," she chirped, hoping to lighten his mood.

He grunted in response, his eyes flicking over to Balin before settling on Ramona.

"What were you two talking about?" he asked, warming his hands by the fire.

"Just discussing the curse," Ramona said, her eyes meeting his. "And Isa."

Thallan's expression darkened at the mention of her name. "What about her?"

"We were just discussing her progress in adjusting to life here," Balin said, sensing the tension in the air. "She seems to be doing well."

Thallan grunted again but didn't say anything else. He moved over to the counter and poured himself a glass of juice, avoiding eye contact with Ramona and Balin.

After a few moments of uncomfortable silence, Ramona decided to speak up. "Thallan, may I ask you something?"

He looked at her, his expression guarded. "What?"

"Why didn't you kill Isa?"

Thallan's jaw tightened at the question. Why was everyone asking him that? He took a sip of juice, buying himself some time to formulate a response.

"Because it wouldn't have been the right thing to do," he finally said.

"But why her specifically?" Ramona pressed, sensing that there was more to the story. "You haven't refrained from killing anyone else."

Thallan let out a heavy sigh, setting down his glass. "You know how I feel about killing women."

"But is that all? Was there no other reason?"

He hesitated. "I knew she wasn't as bad as the letter said. The curse may force me to kill, but I don't like to kill the innocent. That's all."

With that, he turned and left the kitchen, his tired footsteps whispering through the halls. A bloody handprint marred the glass he left behind.

Isa stood on a balcony, looking out over the city below. It was a beautiful sight, illuminated by a thousand twinkling lights and the stars that shone brightly in the night sky.

She sighed contentedly, feeling the cool night air on her skin. She had been waiting all day for this moment when the sun finally set, and the sky bathed everything in shades of purple and pink. She could feel the tension of the day melting away with each passing minute.

Suddenly, Isa felt a presence behind her, and before she had time to react, a pair of strong arms wrapped around her waist. Startled, she turned to look at who it was that had disturbed her peaceful moment. Standing there was a man, tall with broad shoulders and long silver hair. He looked like he could have come from one of the old paintings of the Mathyran heroes that hung in her grandparents' house. His gaze was inviting and kind as he smiled down at her warmly. They stood there for a moment, looking out over the city together, Isa's head leaning against his chest.

The man's touch was familiar and comforting. She felt safe and content, held gently in his warm embrace. He rested his chin on her head while his fingers lightly caressed her arms. His heart beat rhythmically against her ear, and the scent of woodsmoke and spice pervaded her senses.

He nuzzled his nose into her hair and breathed in deeply. Then, he tenderly kissed her neck, sending shivers down her spine. Isa closed her eyes and enjoyed the moment of pure bliss. She almost forgot the city below as they stood entwined on the balcony with magic filling the night air—the magic that only two lovers can feel when they are together.

But then, something changed. The air grew cold, and the sky darkened ominously. The man's arms tightened around her, squeezing her in a grasp that was no longer gentle but fierce and possessive. She tried to break free, but he was too strong. Fear began to course through her veins. She was trapped.

Isa's heart pounded as she struggled to escape his powerful hold. She twisted and turned, but he held on, his grip unyielding. Panic set in as she realized she was in danger, trapped in the arms of a stranger who had suddenly turned hostile.

She bit her lip hard, tasting the metallic tang of blood as she tried to scream for help. But no sound escaped her throat. She looked behind her, and what she saw chilled her to the bone. The man's silver hair had turned black, and his once-kind gaze had transformed into a dark, sinister stare.

Just then, he moved. She felt him pick her up, and he held her high in the air while a menacing laugh erupted from his lips and echoed across the city. She didn't dare move, for he held her over the balcony railing, and the drop to the ground below suddenly appeared infinite.

With a last evil chortle, he released her. She felt the air rush past her as she plummeted toward the earth below. Terror filled her. Her heart pounded, and her breath caught in her throat.

And then, with a gasp, Isa woke. It was just a dream. Still, the fear lingered in her heart. She felt a dull ache in her chest as the vision faded away, leaving a sense of loss behind. She missed the intimacy she had felt with her dream Thallan, but she couldn't ignore the reminder of his ferocity and the elves' cruelty.

The Dark Blade watched from the shadows at the entrance to the city. The night was still and silent, and the last rays of the setting sun glinted off the braces of the gates as they stood open. The Blade felt the familiar thrill of anticipation as he waited for the other assassin to appear.

While the Beast's story certainly sounded plausible, he must be sure before returning to his employer. So, despite the danger, he had decided to try again. However, he would search when the Beast wasn't around this time. He didn't relish another encounter with that man.

At last, a shadow emerged from between the trees and stepped through the gateway. The

158

Dark Blade's heart raced with excitement as he recognized the Beast's tall figure. He melted farther into the shadows and waited for his adversary to pass. With the Beast out of the way, the Blade stepped from his hiding place and headed into the forest, taking the same path he had traveled when he followed the man before.

He couldn't see any tracks in the moonlight, but he trusted his instincts. He stopped occasionally to listen for signs of life, but there was nothing. When he arrived at the location where he had previously encountered the assassin, he paused and studied the area carefully. Only a few scuff marks were visible where he had gone down and then attempted to fight off his attacker.

The Dark Blade straightened up and looked around. Here is where his search would begin. There was one question he had to answer first. Why did the Beast attack him here?

Was it because he'd just realized he was being followed? If that were the case, then the direction they had been walking was probably the correct one. However, if he'd discovered he was being followed earlier, he could have been leading him astray from the moment he noticed his presence. The assassin crossed his arms and considered the question. Finally, he decided that his best course of action would be to continue in the direction they had been headed.

So, he proceeded on that path, moving deeper into the forest. The trees became thicker and taller as he went, blocking out the moonlight and obscuring his vision. The shadows shifted and danced, making it impossible to see where he was going. The Blade was beginning to lose hope when, at last, he spotted a faint light in the distance. He moved closer, and soon, he could make out an old, crumbling manor. A dim, orange glow shone from a side window.

He crept closer, staying in the shadows, and peered through the glass. Inside, he saw Isabella sitting at a table, shelling beans. She was talking to another woman who stood by the fire, stirring something in a pot. So, she did live. He was glad he had decided to double-check.

The Blade would have made a move then. It would have been so easy; she was right there. Even the presence of the other woman wouldn't have stopped him. If it weren't for the man. That was different.

In the corner, sharpening a blade, sat an elf. His pointed ears poked out from his long blonde hair. Even sitting, it was clear that he was tall and broad. A typical elf. Similar to the build of the Beast. That's when everything finally made sense. That was why the Beast was so good at his job. That's why he realized the Dark Blade was following him when no one had ever detected him before. He was an elf.

The assassin knew he didn't stand a chance against that man, and if the height and beauty of the other woman were any indication, she was probably an elf, too. While she might be a challenge, he felt he could handle her, but not with the male elf there.

The Blade quickly backed away and ducked into the trees. He'd found Isabella, but he knew he would have to wait before making a move. The Beast should be returning soon, and he didn't want to be anywhere in the area when he made an appearance.

Chapter 9

Isa walked through the grand doorway of the dining hall, her feet sinking into the deep, lush carpet. Thallan was already there, waiting at the table. She hesitated. Her stomach knotted as she approached. She didn't know if this was a good idea. Their last attempt at dinner hadn't gone well.

She attempted to recall the pleasant conversations she'd heard her father engage in during court functions—conversations that were carefully constructed to avoid any real depth. He always said it was more difficult for someone to find something to argue about when you kept the topics light. Though, some people could argue about anything.

However, if you really cared about getting to know someone, you had to risk the dangers of depth. Genuine relationships couldn't take root in shallow soil. Did she care about getting to know Thallan? He certainly intrigued her, but did she want to risk heartbreak for a man who didn't appear capable of feeling any emotion other than anger?

She had told Ramona she would try, so she would try.

Thallan glanced up as she walked in, his face stoic. He was still dressed all in black, and she could see his dagger at his hip, a weapon that, according to etiquette rules, he was not supposed to bring to the table. Isa swallowed and forced a smile, hoping she could make this dinner better than the last one.

"Good evening, Thallan," she said, gliding into her chair.

"Good evening."

Their eyes met briefly, the silence between them awkward and tense. Isa had to break it.

"So," she began, her voice a little too loud in the silence of the room. She reached for the container of soup and scooped some into her bowl, her mind scrambling for a topic of conversation. People generally liked to talk about themselves, so she'd start there.

"Tell me about your childhood before you joined the elven military."

Thallan's eyes widened slightly, and he seemed to tense even more.

"It was pleasant." His tone contained an air of finality, and he immediately began eating. Clearly, he didn't want her to press the issue, so she didn't.

Very well, then, she'd be the first to lower her walls. One of them had to do it. It might as well be her. In the physical realm, she had no chance of facing him as an equal. But she was a woman, and women were accustomed to fighting in the emotional realm. She was strong in that world—strong enough to take the risk of being the first to open up. If he rejected her, she'd deal with it and move on. If not...

She decided she would tell him about her own childhood. It had been wonderful growing up in the court, living in the castle. The only blight on her memories was the princess. Their mutual dislike did add a bit of a sour taste to what would otherwise have been a pleasant youth. However, Isa had plenty of happy memories she could share. So, as they ate their delicious meal, Isa talked.

For the most part, Thallan ignored her, but Isa could occasionally see a hint of interest in his eyes. She shared stories of playing in the castle gardens, running through the castle hallways, getting into mischief with the other children.

She found herself relaxing as she spoke, the stories and memories tumbling out of her like water from a pitcher. She told him about the time she had snuck into the kitchen and stolen a pastry, only to be caught by the head chef. She told him about the time she had convinced her nursemaid to let her stay up all night to stargaze and how she had fallen asleep in the garden and woken up covered in dew.

Thallan listened to her tales, his expression softening as she spoke, and Isa found herself drawn to him, the air between them no longer tense. As the night wore on, they began to relax in each other's company, their meal long gone. Thallan listened intently now, his eyes never leaving her face. When she finally ran out of stories, he nodded slowly as if processing everything she had said.

"It sounds like you had an entertaining childhood."

Isa felt her cheeks flush with pleasure. She smiled shyly in response, unable to think of anything else to say.

"My past was a bit more unusual," he continued, his voice soft and measured. "I was the third son. My eldest brothers had other duties and didn't spend much time with me, and my younger sister had her own friends. I never really felt like I fit in with any of them."

Isa nodded sympathetically. Growing up around the princess and her entourage, she could relate to that feeling of not entirely belonging.

"I used to spend a lot of time alone as a child," Thallan continued, "exploring in the woods and learning about plants and animals." He paused for a moment. When he spoke again, it was with an air of resignation. "Then, when I got older, I joined the military, and the resulting curse led me here."

Isa smiled sadly at him across the table. She knew how hard the decision must have been for him to leave his kingdom, but she also understood why he couldn't stay. She wanted to reach out and offer him comfort, but she recognized that he didn't appreciate physical contact from her. Instead, she simply said, "I'm sorry."

Then Thallan opened up a little more, telling her about his training for the military, the harsh discipline, and the intense physical preparation he had undergone to become the deadly warrior he was today. Isa listened in fascination, her eyes wide as he spoke of the many battles he had fought, the journeys he had been on, and the various people he had encountered throughout his life.

There was something about the elf that she found herself drawn to, something about his strength and quiet intensity that called to her on a deeper level. The conversation between them flowed easily now, no longer awkward or stilted. The hours flew by quickly, and Isa couldn't remember ever having had a more pleasant evening as they talked late into the night. When finally, it was time for them to part ways, Isa was surprised at how much she'd enjoyed being in the assassin's company.

She only felt slightly disappointed when he headed out the front door instead of toward his rooms. She knew where he was going and why. A burst of determination surged through her as she watched him leave. She *would* break his curse. She would free him from this insatiable need to destroy.

She practically ran to his chambers. She hadn't discovered anything helpful in the library. Ramona wouldn't tell her anything. Thallan wouldn't tell her anything. Maybe he had something in his rooms.

She would look there. She hastily pushed down the surge of guilt that arose. She wouldn't invade his privacy any more than she had to— *as she rummaged through all his belongings*, she thought with a twinge.

She opened the door to his chambers and glanced around. She didn't dare light a candle, even though he would probably be gone for hours, that is, if tonight was like the other nights. Still, she didn't want to take the chance that Ramona or Balin would see. She would have to search by the light of the fire in the fireplace.

The room was surprisingly neat, with everything in its place. Nothing obvious stood out—no artifacts or magic potions that could hold the answer she sought. Several leather-bound books filled a bookshelf on one wall, and Isa flipped through them all. They were filled with pages upon pages of notes on various plants and animals, but she could find nothing related to curses or magic within their folds.

She scoured every nook and cranny, looking for anything remotely magical or out of the ordinary. No luck. Frustrated, Isa turned to his wardrobe.

Thallan entered the town silently, his feet making no more noise than a whisper on the cobblestones. Even though he moved swiftly, he was still careful to stay in the shadows, his movements as graceful as those of a cat. He could feel an energy in the air, an electricity that seemed to linger even in the darkness of night.

A chill ran down his spine as he passed through the gates as if an unseen force was watching him. His eyes searched the area, but he saw nothing more than the usual collection of homeless people loitering nearby.

He shook off the feeling, dismissing it. He would deal with it later if it turned out to be anything significant. He had a job to do now.

He made his way down the dark alley. With each step, the feeling he had by the gate lingered in the back of his mind. He glanced around, searching for the source of his unease, but he couldn't see anyone. Once again, he pushed it away and focused on the task at hand.

His destination was a house on the far side of the alley, and he made his way there quickly. A sense of urgency encompassed him, and his emotions, which the magic usually kept buried, seemed to be struggling to rise to the surface.

He exhaled slowly, his nerves tense. He took a few steps forward, caution growing with each step. Stopping at the edge of the alley, he peered around the corner to ensure the coast was clear.

Darkness enveloped him as he moved forward, and a feeling of dread washed over him. What was happening? He didn't believe it could be related to the contract he was about to fulfill. The aura of impending doom felt larger than that—more life-altering. More devastating.

Something else was going on. He had to finish this quickly. For finish it, he must. The curse wouldn't release him from its clutches just because something felt strange. He hurried on.

He finally reached the back of the house and waited a few moments to ensure no one had seen him. Everything was quiet. He moved to the door, his eyes darting around the area as he searched for any sign of danger.

He couldn't thoroughly shake his growing nervousness, but he shoved it aside, focusing on his mission. He quickly opened the door, keeping his movements as stealthy as possible.

Once he had slipped inside the building, the harsh sound of his target's voice hit him. Without hesitation, Thallan drew his blade and stepped forward to meet him. He slashed through the air and buried his sword in the man's stomach.

His face remained passive as blood poured between his fingers. He still felt nothing when executing his targets. Even with the new emotions that had been attempting to rise in him lately, guilt, remorse, empathy, those were not present.

As he finished the job, he rushed from the house, not taking the time to be as cautious as usual. Flying through the forest, he rapidly made his way back to his manor. The sense of unease grew with every step.

He quickly searched the house, finding Ramona and Balin relaxing in the kitchen as usual. They glanced up at him curiously when he burst into the room.

"What's wrong," asked Balin.

"I don't know. Where's Isa?"

Ramona raised her brows in concern. "She should be in her rooms."

Thallan closed his eyes and reached out with his elven magic, searching for the collection of water molecules he had come to recognize as hers.

Startled, he realized she was in his chambers. Alarmed as to what she could be doing there, he rushed to his rooms. He crossed the sitting room and moved into his bedroom, slinging the door wide.

To his dismay, he saw Isa standing before the wardrobe, reaching out a finger only inches away from his magical rose.

She stopped when she saw him, guilt etched across her face. She bit her lip before finally admitting, "I was looking for some clue as to how to break the curse, and I found this. What is it?" She watched the rose pulse brightly in the darkness of the closet.

It was not supposed to pulse. What had the woman done? Fury raged through him. He had trusted her. They had just had a pleasant evening where he'd felt they had developed mutual respect and had even bonded in a small way. And now, here she was, invading his privacy and threatening his most valuable possession.

She was only a breath away from the magical flower. It was the only thing that allowed him any semblance of control over the curse—over his emotions. Without it, the anger and rage that accompanied the goblin's revenge would consume him.

Had she touched it? Had she disturbed it at all? It was so fragile. Even the most minor interference could weaken it, and it couldn't be mended or replaced. So much depended on that rose. It was the only thing preventing him from losing control and killing everyone.

"How dare you!" he yelled, his voice echoing off the walls.

Isa shrank away from Thallan's anger. There was no buried gentleness behind that outburst. No subtle hint of a hidden restraint like she had detected before.

Only rage.

Pure, unadulterated rage.

Her entire body shook with a fear that his voice seemed to grab and rip up from her inner being. She opened her mouth to speak, but no words came out. Images from her dream forced their way into her head, and the man before her seemed to morph into the monster of her nightmare.

Thallan glared at her and stepped closer, towering over her small frame. "Were you trying to destroy me? Destroy us all?"

"No! I-I'm sorry," Isa stammered, tears welling in her eyes. Where was the elf she'd just shared dinner with? Where was the understanding and willingness to listen that she had spent the last several hours enjoying? What had become of her gentle assassin? She felt her heart crack.

"I was just so desperate to find a way to break the curse. I wanted to help you. I didn't mean any harm."

Thallan growled at her. "I should have killed you in your room that first night."

Isa's heart dropped to her stomach. She understood he was angry, but she never expected him to say something so cruel, not now. She took a step back, her legs trembling. "Please, Thallan. I'm sorry. I swear I won't do it again."

The swirling red whisps of magic that made up the floating rose flickered. Thallan's eyes darkened, and Isa could feel the growing rage emanating from him. "You betrayed my trust, Isa." He stepped even closer to her, his breath hot on her face. "How can I ever trust you again?"

Isa's knees went weak, and she fell to the ground. "Please," she begged, not sure what she was asking for.

His mercy.

His forgiveness.

His transformation back into the elf he was before—the elf she was beginning to know and care for.

Thallan glared down at her, his silver-rimmed blue eyes flashing with anger and betrayal. She recoiled at the coldness radiating from them. What had she done? Why had she allowed her blind determination to destroy what they had begun to build between them?

Thallan turned away, his anger still boiling inside him. He took a deep breath before glancing at her over his shoulder. "Go," he said, his voice low and menacing. "I don't want to see you here again."

Isa didn't need to be told twice. She jumped to her feet and quickly made her escape, leaving the man alone in his chambers.

⚭⚭⚭

Thallan roared. He pulled his swords free and swung them at the bedpost, severing it neatly into three pieces.

Balin watched from the doorway.

"Ramona won't thank you for destroying the furniture."

"Then give me something better to destroy."

Balin drew his blade and twirled it so the tip traced ovals in the air.

The two of them began to circle one another, weapons clashing in a rhythmic tempo. Sweat formed on Balin's forehead as he fought to keep up with Thallan's agility and skill. Gradually, the pace of their duel increased until they were both lunging and slashing at each other at speeds human eyes wouldn't be able to follow.

Balin blocked blow after blow, parrying some strikes while dodging others, but slowly began to tire as the minutes dragged on. He could feel Thallan pushing him back, taking every advantage he could find.

"What's gotten you so fierce tonight?" Balin asked, barely blocking a downward swing before it cut his head in two. "You seem unusually agitated, even given the situation."

Thallan pressed his lips together tightly. "Isa." He shook his head. "I don't know. She was standing by the rose. I don't *know*. I haven't felt such fury since before the fairy crafted the subduing magic for me."

"Do you think she did something to it?"

"I can't be sure, but it seemed to...waver."

"What was she looking for?" Balin asked, jumping back to avoid having his legs chopped off at the knees.

"She claimed," Thallan spit out, "she was looking for information on the curse. She says she wants to help me break it."

"And you don't believe her?" Balin grunted as he swung his sword up to block Thallan's blade coming toward his neck.

"Oh, I believe her." Thallan spun, twirling both swords above his head and bringing them around at Balin, lightning fast, strike after strike after strike. It was all Balin could do to keep Thallan's blades from mortally wounding him.

"It doesn't change anything," Thallan said through gritted teach. "Even ignoring the damage she could have done to the rose, she still broke into my chambers when I was gone and went through my belongings. That is unacceptable. Even Ramona doesn't disturb my things when she cleans. There is no excuse for such boorish behavior."

"Perhaps," suggested Balin, breathing heavily, "perhaps, human customs are different."

"Not so different," Thallan said with a grunt as he crossed his swords to stop a downward strike from Balin. "She at least had the grace to sound regretful, and she apologized. A person doesn't do that unless they know they are in the wrong."

"Look, I understand you're angry," Balin said, spinning away from a low-swinging blade. "And you have every right to be, but Isa was only trying to help you. Her motives are noble, even if her methods are a bit misguided and dangerous."

Thallan snorted. "A bit misguided? A *bit* dangerous? If she'd damaged the magic, I could have gone berserk. I still might. I don't know what she did, but I certainly don't feel normal right now."

Balin smiled. "I don't know much about the girl, but based on what Ramona has said, I'm sure any damage wasn't intentional. Perhaps," he said with a groan as Thallan's kick hit home across his thigh. "Perhaps you should give her another chance."

Thallan stilled, his blades held down by his sides. Balin stumbled at the sudden cessation of their fight.

"Why?"

"Well, Ramona has a theory, though, I'm sure you won't like it."

Thallan quirked a brow.

"She thinks you're beginning to fall in love with the human, and the curse is reacting with increased potency and acting on your emotions, as well, to keep you two apart."

"That's ridiculous," Thallan said, crossing his arms. "It's not as if the curse were sentient." He glanced around the room at the visions of his victims that still followed him everywhere he went. Was it?

"Even if the curse is under that misguided notion," he said, "that's even more reason for me to stay away from her. If she leaves, things can go back to how they were."

Balin carefully studied his friend. "Do you really want things to return to how they were?"

Thallan imagined a life without Isa in it. Loneliness and sorrow ate through the rage that had been burning within him. No. That wasn't what he wanted.

"Fine," he said, turning and walking away. "I'll go talk to her."

"Deep, calming breaths first," reminded Balin as he headed out the door.

Chapter 10

Isa sprinted out of the house, her heart pounding and her mind in turmoil. She stumbled over a stray vine in the overgrown garden, falling to her knees. For the longest time, she just knelt there, sobbing into her hands. She shouldn't have gone through his room. Even as she did it, she had known that it was wrong.

Still, did he have to react so harshly? She groaned. She had started to really care for him despite her better judgment. She no longer saw her father's murderers when she looked at him. She saw him, with his positive attributes and his flaws. But now, it didn't matter. She had ruined it.

There was nothing left for her here, only pain and sorrow. She had to get away, to put as much distance between herself and Thallan as possible. She pushed herself to her feet. She didn't stop to think; she just ran.

A dark shape stood amid the trees surrounding the dwelling and watched Isa pass. As silently as a phantom, he slipped through the forest after her.

The Blade hadn't made a move while she wept in the garden, and he'd still bide his time until he had put considerable distance between them and the manor. He didn't dare risk Thallan or the other male elf discovering him and intervening.

Soon enough, Isa stopped her mad dash. Sitting on a fallen log, she tried to catch her breath. Tears streaked down her face, and, once more, sobs wracked her body. She dropped her face into her hands again and let herself cry, mourning the loss of what might have been.

The Blade watched her and hardened his heart against the sight. She was a target, nothing else. He intentionally stepped on a twig to frighten her. He always got a thrill from the fear his victims experienced just before their inevitable demise.

Isa jumped at the sound and whipped her head around, trying desperately to see in the dim light of the forest. A man dressed all in black stepped out from behind the trees. Instead of running, she only stared at him, thinking, for a moment, that it was Thallan. But then she realized the man before her was too short to be her elf. He also lacked the broad shoulders and the twin blades. Another assassin. Princess Nixa had sent someone else after her, and they'd found her.

Isa let out a piercing scream as she flew through the forest. Panic propelled her to near-superhuman speeds. Twigs and branches tore at her exposed skin with searing pain as she sped forward, not daring to look back.

Suddenly, her ankle twisted on a rock, and a wave of agony crashed over her as she slammed into the unforgiving ground.

The Blade descended upon her with terrifying speed, his sword poised to snuff out her life. Her cry cut through the air, raw with terror, regret, and despair.

He raised his sword, the dark steel glinting in the moonlight. At that moment, Isa thought she was surely dead. Thallan's face flashed through her mind, and she wished she had one more chance to save him.

Just as the Blade was about to strike, a roar reverberated through the trees. A mass of black flew towards him and blocked his sword with a force that sent him flying backward with a cry of disbelief.

Thallan stood with his back to her, brandishing his blades, his fierce visage trained on the other assassin. The Dark Blade raised his sword to strike, but Thallan brought up his own in a swift parry. Sparks flew in the night as their swords clashed again and again.

Streaks of blood began to appear all over the Blade's body, soaking his clothes and flying out to color the grass around them. Thallan was playing with him. Or punishing him. The sound of metal rang through the forest as the elf pressed forward relentlessly until his assault knocked the other man to the ground. He slashed out with his sword as he fell, landing a lucky strike on Thallan's arm. It didn't even slow the elf down.

Isa looked on in shock, her ankle forgotten in the heat of the moment. Thallan leaned over the Dark Blade, his sword held steady. The other assassin tried to scramble away, but Thallan was too fast. He grasped the Blade by the collar, pulling him to his feet.

"Who sent you?" Thallan growled, his eyes blazing with fury.

The Dark Blade only sneered, refusing to answer. Thallan shook him hard, making him gasp for air.

"Who sent you?" he repeated, his voice low and dangerous.

Finally, the assassin relented. "You know I can't tell you that," he spat. "Probably, the same one who sent you after the girl the first time."

Thallan's grip tightened as he glared at the other man. Isa could read in his eyes what he was about to do. She turned her head away and squeezed her eyes closed.

Thallan released the man, and he fell to the ground, but he had no time to run. In a single, smooth motion, Thallan brought up his sword and swept it across the Dark Blade's neck. The man who had come for Isa lay dead on the forest floor.

Thallan replaced his blades and turned to Isa with a sad smile. His eyes traveled to her torn dress and scratched body. Without a word, he leaned down and carefully picked her up. Her eyes shot to his in surprise. Why was he treating her so gently now after their recent thunderous argument? She didn't complain. Whatever had possessed him was gone now. They could address it later. She wrapped her arms around his neck and watched his face as he slowly walked back to the manor.

Silence covered them as Thallan carried Isa back home. And she was glad. She didn't want

179

the distraction words would bring. She was enjoying being wrapped in the cocoon of his embrace with the feel of his muscles beneath her and his chest rising and falling against her side. The scent of his skin, crisp and clean, enveloped her. For a moment, Isa forgot about the danger that had just passed and let herself be lulled by Thallan's steady heartbeat and the rhythmic sound of his breath.

Finally, they reached Isa's chambers. Thallan set her down carefully on the bed, his hand lingering on her waist for a second longer than necessary. Isa looked up at him, her eyes meeting his.

"Thank you," she whispered, trying to convey her immense gratitude in those simple words.

Thallan only nodded, his eyes unreadable, before he turned and walked away. Isa watched him go, her heart heavy with a mix of emotions. She lay back on her bed and tried to sort through the jumbled mess of her thoughts.

As she lay there, the pain in her ankle and the wounds from the forest began to throb. She also realized with a start that she was still wearing the elaborate gown she had worn to dinner, now ripped beyond repair. Ramona would kill her.

She sat up slowly, wincing in pain as her ankle protested the movement. She knew she needed to change her clothes and tend to her wounds, but she would probably need help.

Just as she was about to call for Ramona, Thallan re-entered the room with a healer's bag in hand. Isa's heart skipped a beat at the sight of him.

Thallan set the bag on the bed and knelt beside her. "Let me take care of you," he said softly.

Isa nodded, unable to form words as he started to tend to her wounds. The heat from his hands sent her pulse racing as he cleaned her cuts and wrapped her ankle with gentle precision.

"What happened out there?" Thallan asked.

Isa took a deep breath before telling him of her mad dash from the manor. Thallan's eyes blazed with fury at the realization of how close that man had come to harming her.

When she finished, he gripped her face and stared deeply into her eyes. "As long as you're under my protection, I won't let anything happen to you," he said fiercely. She didn't understand this sudden change in him. His attitude now fit more with the Thallan she had begun to get to know at dinner than the one she had encountered later in his quarters.

"Why are you being so nice to me?" she asked.

"I may get angry with you occasionally," he said, "but you are one of us as long as you are here. Fleeting emotions don't change how we care for our own."

Isa's heart swelled at his words, and she felt a warmth spread through her body. Though she suspected there was more to his recent outburst than that, she didn't press the issue. She simply nodded, unable to speak, as she gazed into his eyes.

Thallan slowly pulled away and stood up, taking a few steps back from the bed. That was when Isa noticed the blood seeping through a cut in his sleeve—a reminder of the fight he had just gone through for her.

"You're hurt!" she exclaimed, panicking as she gestured to his wound. "Let me take care of it."

Thallan hesitated before shrugging off his shirt. It was minor. It would heal on its own, but he liked the idea of Isa tending to his wounds, wounds he had received protecting her. There was something primal and satisfying in the thought.

Isa gasped at the sight of the scars that lined his arms and torso. He may have had the healing power of an elf, but apparently, that didn't mean all reminders of his injuries vanished. She quickly collected herself and grabbed the bag.

Isa's breath felt heavy as Thallan sat beside her on the bed. She tried to keep her eyes on his wound and not let them stray to the toned muscles under her hands. But no matter how much she tried, she couldn't ignore how his bare skin felt against her fingers as she worked. Every touch sent a jolt of electricity through her body.

Thallan watched her with a mix of amusement and longing in his eyes. Isa knew she shouldn't be thinking about him this way, but she couldn't help it. Being so close to him, feeling the heat of his body and the strength and power he possessed, was driving her crazy. Finally, she tied off the bandage and sat back, watching him intently.

"Thallan, I really am sorry about searching your room without permission and then putting you in danger by recklessly running away like that. You had warned me about the possibility of other assassins being out there, and I didn't listen. Thank you for saving my life again."

Thallan heaved a great sigh. "I understand. You desire to help free me." He ran his knuckles down her cheek. "I should not have reacted the way I did. For that, I apologize."

Isa smiled at him, tears pooling in her eyes.

Thallan stood up and pulled his shirt back on, his eyes never leaving hers. "Rest now," he said softly, tucking a strand of hair behind her ear. "You're safe within these walls."

Isa closed her eyes and let herself drift off to sleep, a smile on her face.

Thallan frowned. The phantoms floated around him in a macabre dance. They surrounded him, blocking his view of the bookshelves he was searching. He could still ignore them; however, he also felt the all too familiar low throb beginning to build in the back of his head. *That* was not as easy to ignore. His urge to kill had started to grow already, and night had not even fallen yet.

The episodes were occurring closer together and becoming more intense. He had barely made it to town the previous night before the drive nearly overcame him. He'd had to expend a tremendous effort to retain control of his mind and suppress the urge long enough to reach his target's house. He'd almost not made it in time.

His actions that night could have easily resulted in a murder spree with over half the city slaughtered. As it was, he hadn't taken the time to scout out the area or verify the number of guards before he snuck in through a window.

He walked through a phantom that wore the face of one of the men he had recently dispatched. Its body evaporated as he passed through it but immediately reformed behind him. They were all there, all of the guards he'd had to eradicate the night before. They all sneered at him.

He didn't spare them a glance as he moved to another bookshelf. Last night's operation had been messy without his usual preparation, and he'd had to destroy so many. He shuddered as he stared at a book, unable to focus enough to read its title.

Even after all the lives he had taken that night, the urge to kill had not been completely satisfied. The darkness inside him lingered like an insatiable beast that could never be tamed. And now, it was returning even earlier than usual. He would need to leave soon, but not yet.

Thallan wandered through the library in silent desperation, searching for anything to help him fight these increasingly violent urges that were slowly taking over. Was Ramona right? Could the curse somehow feel his growing attachment to Isa? Or had the girl damaged the magical rose somehow and weakened its power?

He had just about given up when he stumbled upon a dusty old volume tucked away in the corner. He pulled it out to better read the faded title, *The Kill Curse*. He gasped. Why was this here and not with the other books on curses?

Thallan felt a spark of hope as he grabbed the ancient tome and pulled it from the shelf. He opened the book and began to read, his eyes widening as he devoured its contents. The book was filled with stories of men cursed by powerful magic-wielders. Men who could no longer control the urges to kill that came over them. Men like him.

He took the book over to a seat by the fireplace and read. The throbbing in his head subsided momentarily as if the curse approved of his current activity.

Some men in the stories managed to break the curse; others didn't. Many of those who didn't had names that struck a familiar chord with Thallan—names of mass murders, tyrants, evil dictators, feared despots. They were infamous for their cruelty and bloodlust.

The others, those who were not so well known, had vanished into the mountains or deep forests and slowly lost their minds, their stories only known from the journals they had kept and that faithful friends had retrieved after their deaths. Some of them had died gradually, no longer able to care for themselves after their minds had snapped, and others had taken their own lives when they felt they could no longer stay isolated from society—when they thought they could no longer keep themselves from giving into the curse entirely.

Would Thallan share that destiny? Was that to be his fate? He shuddered at the thought. Was he already beginning to lose his mind now that the urges were growing stronger and more frequent?

As he continued to read, he started to understand what was happening to him now. Ramona had been right. His newfound feelings for Isa had triggered a response in the curse that was slowly taking hold of him, pushing him closer and closer to a path of destruction and violence. Something would happen soon. Either the curse would break, or he would break. He'd have to leave.

Could Isa help him break the curse? He didn't even attempt to deny the feelings he had for her. There was no point. The curse knew, or it wouldn't respond the way it was. Yes, he had strong feelings, but was it love?

He admired her kindness and generosity, even to those she deemed unworthy. He respected her courage and determination. He was impressed by her willingness to do whatever it took to reach her goals, regardless of the pain or suffering she might endure. He was glad she didn't compromise and take the easy way out.

They shared many values and interests, as he'd learned from their talk at dinner. He enjoyed her company. He liked how she got a little crease between her eyes when she thought deeply about something, and, yes, he was attracted to her. Very much so. She was constantly on his mind, and there were times when he wanted to reach out and touch her so badly that he thought he would go mad if he didn't. He also felt fiercely protective of her. He would rather die than see any harm come to her. Was that what love was?

She was a human. Though that thought didn't hold the same amount of disgust it had in the past. The distinction actually didn't seem to matter even as he thought it. He shook his head and stared into the flames.

He remembered the feeling he'd gotten when he found her water signature deep in the forest, being followed by the other presence. When he'd heard her scream. The anger that had consumed him remained, but it had instantly switched its focus. Panic and fear had risen to join it. Isa couldn't die.

Everything he'd just been enraged at her for immediately lost all importance. She was the only thing that mattered. Everything else was immaterial. She had to live. He couldn't survive without her.

Yes.

He had to admit it to himself.

He loved her.

Thallan sighed. Even so, she could never love him. He would never forget her reaction after discovering he was an elf. Her hatred as she pummeled him. What she had said about how elven warriors had tortured her father. No, she could never love an elf assassin like him.

He would have to leave in order to keep them all safe. Thallan groaned in despair as he realized that he couldn't leave either. He had killed the Dark Blade, but whoever hired him would send others when he didn't return. He had to get Isa out of here first before he could even think of disappearing himself. In the meantime, he should avoid her as much as possible. It would be easier to retain control if thoughts of the human didn't constantly run through his mind.

The curse flared up again as if angry at being kept waiting. The sun had still not set, but Thallan knew he couldn't postpone it any longer.

187

Jumping up from his seat, he gently placed the book on a table and hurried out.

Isa twirled in the hallways, her soft yellow gown swishing with her every move.

Singing quietly, she opened doors as she explored the large mansion. She had not taken much time to look around before, and she felt her ever-present curiosity flare to life when she realized that she might be able to find some clue to the curse somewhere else in this vast home. Probably not, but it was possible.

She wouldn't enter anyone's personal rooms, not anymore, but she could search through the common spaces. She didn't know what she expected to find, mayhap an abandoned book or a vial with a label that said, "Drink this to break a curse." She chuckled lightly at the thought. That would be nice. But even if she didn't find anything, she had to look. Otherwise, she would never know.

She'd been exploring the manor for hours, discovering empty sleeping quarters, vacant sitting rooms, and forgotten closets. When she opened the next door, a brilliant wash of sunlight hit her face. It illuminated an endless sea of treasures—crystal chandeliers, fine tapestries hanging on the walls, and rows of beautiful instruments.

Lady Isabella stepped into the grand ballroom and gasped at the sheer size of it. Her eyes trailed up to the mural-painted ceilings, and she marveled at the vast windows that bathed the space in a soft, magical light. Everywhere she looked, the crystal chandeliers glimmered against the walls and reflected off the highly polished dance floor below. As her eyes traveled around, she noticed the balconies and mezzanines that lined either side of the ballroom, offering a beautiful bird's-eye view of all the festivities below.

She could imagine standing at one of those high vantage points, watching as couples twirled and swayed to music. Isa was so taken by the sheer beauty of it all she couldn't help but laugh and run into the center of the polished dance floor. This was familiar. She hadn't realized how much she missed it.

She twirled and spun to a tune only she could hear, her gown flaring out in a blur of yellow as she whirled around. It was exhilarating to be all alone in such an impressive space. A sense of freedom surged through her. She let go of all her worries, flinging them away as she swirled around the room.

Isa's senses must have grown sharper since she'd been living with the elves. Because as she danced, she noticed that the air seemed to shift as if magic were at work. She paused in her twirling and looked around, wondering if perhaps she had been caught in some spell. Then, she saw him, her handsome elf, standing on the other side of the ballroom, his long silver hair hanging loose around his shoulders, and his piercing eyes turned her way.

Thallan leaned against the wall with his arms crossed over his broad chest. A plethora of emotions hit her: shock, embarrassment, the slight thrill of excitement that always seemed to accompany his presence. She smiled.

Thallan had been trying to avoid the girl and banish her from his thoughts. Perhaps, then, the curse would let up some. Perhaps he could better focus on controlling it. *That* was why he'd sent out his magic to see where she was. Not from any desire to stalk her.

The ballroom? What was she doing there? He would go and quickly check on her. As soon as he saw that she was alright, he'd come back and put her out of his mind. Like an addict chasing his addiction, Thallan headed down the hall.

She looked so beautiful. Her eyes were alight with excitement, and joy shone from her face as she moved gracefully around the room.

"You dance well, considering you have no music," he said when she glanced his way.

He took long, slow strides towards her as if he were being pulled against his will. All thoughts of avoiding her fled his mind. He felt like time had turned back, and he stood in the midst of his father's court. Before he saw so much death. Before he was cursed.

He was once again a carefree, happy man, and here before him was a beautiful woman. He felt a sudden desire to dance with her. He wanted to hold her in his arms and pretend that everything would be okay—that they had a chance at a forever together.

He extended his hand. "Would you do me the honor?" he asked, smiling.

Isabella gazed at his face intently as if searching for signs of duplicity. It must seem strange to her. An assassin dancing. But she didn't know all of his history yet. He wanted to

190

tell her. He wanted to share every memory with her, the old and the new.

Thallan breathed a sigh of relief when she accepted his offer, even though her dainty fingers were cold and shook slightly. He noticed the tremor but didn't allow it to penetrate his emotions. After all, it was only natural that she would still fear him after everything she had experienced.

He held her with one hand and waved the other, making the instruments lining the room come to life and fill the air with sweet music.

Thallan watched the kaleidoscope of emotions that played across her face: surprise, joy, and finally, delight. The gentle glow of the chandeliers, that he also brought to life, illuminated her skin, making her almost look like a mythical creature from another world. He suppressed a sigh. She was not a mythical creature; she was human—a human who hated elves. He shook his head to clear his mind of any forbidden thoughts. He would allow himself this moment.

And so, they danced. He held her close as they moved to the tune of the music. The warmth of her in his arms seemed to thaw his cold heart. It felt right. She belonged there. He pulled her closer and held her more tightly. She was his. The thought rippled through him almost savagely. How could he ever have believed he could forget her? Could leave her behind?

She was his life.

His very breath.

Every beat of his heart.

He could not survive without her. Yet, he couldn't take her with him. That left only one option.

The music eventually stopped, and Isa absentmindedly placed her hand on Thallan's chest as she tried to catch her breath. Her cheeks were flushed with color when she looked up at him, and Thallan felt a gentle tenderness spread through his body.

He knew what he would have to do. She may never be able to love him, but her kind, open heart might still sorrow at his demise. He didn't want it to hurt her any more than necessary, so he *would* stay away from her. Not for his sake but for hers. She needed to forget him and move on with her life.

With an inward groan at his lack of restraint, he bowed elaborately.

"Thank you, My Lady, for a most enjoyable dance."

Isa curtsied back, "It was my pleasure, My Lord."

With a sad smile, he turned and left. As he passed the threshold, it felt like a great force brutally ripped his heart from his body. It stayed behind with the human girl.

Chapter 11

Isa had been frequenting the library mainly during the daytime, so Thallan went in the evening, hoping to avoid her. He needed to read more of *The Kill Curse*. He'd planned to grab it quickly and take it back to his rooms; however, when he entered the library, he saw Isa standing before a shelf, flipping through the pages of a book.

He hesitated. Should he leave? She hadn't noticed him. He could still get his book and go before she even realized he was there.

He didn't want to. It wouldn't hurt the girl if he took a second to watch her—to imprint her image in his mind. She needn't even know. Thallan chastised himself. So, now he was nothing more than a stalker.

He moved across the room and picked up his book, making no attempt to be silent. Still, she didn't notice. He smiled indulgently. Humans were so oblivious. He wondered how close he could get to her before she became aware of his presence.

If he intended to assassinate her, he could do so without her ever even knowing he was there, but that was the furthest from his mind. So, he walked normally, watching her for any reaction. Nothing. Stifling a chuckle, Thallan stopped right behind her.

"Hello."

Isa jumped and knocked over a nearby table.

Thallan caught it before it hit the ground and sat it upright. Then he moved in closer, trapping her against the shelf with a hand on either side of her head. He hardly knew what he was doing—acting purely on instinct and emotion. He looked down at her, fascinated by the panic in those wide green eyes.

What caused it? What did she fear? Him? Maybe. Herself? He knew she was attracted to him. Could she fear that she would lose control and give in to her desires? For a second, he allowed himself to dream of the possibility. But the dream was tainted by reality demanding to be heard. He ignored it.

"What are you doing to me?" He whispered, moving closer.

Isa placed both hands on his chest, not completely grasping his shirt, yet not completely pushing him away. Indecision clouded her eyes. Could she be experiencing the same inner turmoil that plagued him?

He instinctively leaned closer. His eyes strayed to her mouth. What would she taste like? He suddenly felt an overwhelming need to know. As if she could read his mind, Isa gasped softly, parting her lips in a move that drew Thallan even closer. Heat rushed through him.

He could feel it in every fiber of his being. It grew into a raging inferno, engulfing him, burning him inside. His head began to pound with the familiar throb, but he hardly noticed. Her breath fanned his skin only millimeters away. He could barely think. He closed the distance and brushed his lips against hers.

The curse instantly reacted. Power emanated from him in waves. His eyes closed off like curtains drawn over a window, his icy blue orbs now rimmed in silver. Thallan felt the storm rising in him. He felt the urge, the need consuming him. He raised his head and stared at Isa.

Some deeply buried instinct told him that he had to get away from her, but he didn't want to leave. He *couldn't* leave. His feet felt rooted to the spot. The fog clouding his mind confused his thoughts.

The library faded from Thallan's vision, and he saw red as he stood on the battleground once more, encompassed by the ghosts of his victims. "Kill." The command was singular, as though all the voices around him spoke at once, and with that single command ringing in his head, Thallan stretched forth his right hand where a sword made of ice and energy materialized.

Pain spread through Isa's body as she was harshly shoved back into the shelf behind her, but her gaze remained on Thallan. She almost didn't recognize her elf. Her eyes widened when she saw the blood dripping from his icy sword. She placed her hands on her mouth to silence the scream that had already bubbled up her throat. But the blood was not hers, nor was it Thallan's.

Balin stood between her and the assassin. Blood ran down his arm, which he had raised to counter Thallan's attack. He moved his hand in a quick succession of gestures, and a colossal plant burst out of the floor and wrapped itself around the manic elf. Thallan glared at his friend murderously.

"I would advise you to move instead of just standing there gawking like a silly girl," Balin said, glancing at Isa over his shoulder.

The annoyance in his voice was difficult to miss, but Isa was too terrified to budge. Her brain told her it was time to run, but she found that her feet were unwilling to cooperate. Balin grunted in frustration. Thallan was already breaking through the temporary restraints, yet Isa couldn't move her eyes away.

"Stubborn human. Ramona'll have my hide if I let anything happen to you," said Balin.

He waved his fingers, and Isa was suddenly wrapped in vines and whisked out of the library. The last thing she saw before the doors closed was the image of Thallan breaking free and swinging wildly for Balin's head.

Isa sat on the floor and gingerly touched her back, the vines falling away. The spot where the shelf had hit her throbbed. As she rubbed it, a disturbing thought materialized. If Balin hadn't pushed her out of the way of Thallan's sword, she would have died.

Thallan would have killed her.

Isa pressed her fingers lightly to her lips, remembering the brief kiss. What had happened? Was it the curse?

A crash sounded from the room, and she pushed herself to her feet. She had to find Ramona. Isa ran through the halls, searching for the only person who could help. Tears gathered in her eyes, but she wiped them off angrily. This was not the time to show weakness.

"You must get to your room," Ramona said, rushing toward her.

"What happened?" Isa asked.

"I don't know, but I felt an enormous rush of power. Something isn't right with Thallan."

"He attacked me in the library," said Isa, clutching her arms across her chest. "Balin came in just in time to stop him, but they're fighting now."

Panic flooded Ramona's face. "Come!" She grabbed Isa and pulled her to her chambers. Isa ran, barely keeping pace with the frantic elf.

Ramona slung Isa's door open. "Stay here," she commanded before slamming it behind the girl. She waved her hands, placing a barrier of light around the entrance. Then she turned on her heels and ran to the library as fast as she could.

The sight that met her eyes when she threw open the doors almost made her heart stop. Balin was bent over, breathing heavily with multiple cuts all over his body. His shirt hung from him in blood-coated tatters.

Her mate was by no means weak, and he was holding his ground, but one look at Thallan told her he couldn't stand for long. The warrior prince was back on the battleground. He had never known defeat, and she doubted he was about to experience it now.

Desperation and determination surged through Ramona as she steadied herself, focusing on the radiant particles of light swirling in the room. She visualized the perfect cage, one large enough to confine Thallan. It would have to be strong. Such a thing wouldn't fit in that room. She needed more space.

"Get him outside, Balin!"

Balin leaped through a nearby window, shards of glass flying in his wake, with Thallan in hot pursuit. Ramona quickly followed, climbing over the sill after them.

Balin led Thallan to a small clearing deep in the woods behind the manor and then distanced himself, creating the necessary space for Ramona to do her work. Thallan stood, glaring at him, as he slowly formed another sword in his other hand.

"Hurry," Balin mumbled through tight lips.

Ramona strained, holding back tears as she quickly channeled immense power into one focused release. Like lightning, it shot out at the crazed elf.

The cage formed around Thallan, enclosing him like a trapped beast. He pounded the energy walls with frantic fury. Ramona's strength wavered as she struggled to maintain the containment. Just when it seemed her core would falter, Balin quietly approached from behind her and placed a hand on her shoulder.

His expression was solemn. She knew he would help her if he could, but their powers were fundamentally different, and any attempt to share his energy would only cause harm. Nevertheless, they stood together, resolute in the face of the daunting task. Ramona continued to draw the shimmering light, reinforcing the cage's structure.

Thallan's power surged. He saw enemies all around him. They taunted him. They lunged at him. Attacked him. He fought madly, striking them down one by one. And still, they came. A bright movement caught his eye, and he glanced up from the carnage surrounding him.

A beautiful lady dressed in a yellow gown danced through the bodies that littered the battleground. Warriors fought and fell everywhere as she gracefully weaved through them. Her long brown hair waved behind her like a flag of victory.

Thallan stared at her, her presence momentarily distracting him from the war raging all around. She danced up to him just as a goblin raised his sword to strike. Flowing around the enemy, she reached Thallan. The blade tore through her as insubstantial as mist.

Enemies swarmed around him, attacking from all sides. Thallan fought back valiantly, striving to protect Isa, but it was unnecessary. None of their weapons could touch her. She smiled and rested her hand on his chest.

"Thallan," she whispered, "come back to me."

Still, the enemy surged.

"Fight it, brother. This is not who you are." Balin's voice came to him as if from the mist.

Thallan turned around, searching for his friend but saw only the dead bodies lying slain on the field, and the ghosts floating in the air. He turned back to the beautiful lady, but Isa no longer stood before him. His eyes shot around frantically and found her in the middle of the field, staring at him. He rushed towards her but couldn't reach her, no matter how fast he moved.

Frustration consumed him. The ice sword in his hand dissolved and splashed to the ground as he let out a roar. The forest around him tremored with the anguished sound.

"In shadows deep and darkness bound,

I curse thee, elf, to the battleground," the voice of the goblin mage echoed in his head.

The old goblin appeared in front of him, his frail shoulders bent. The hair on his head was clumped together with caked blood and stuck to his forehead.

"How long will you punish me for fighting a justified war?" Thallan asked angrily.

The creature glared at him.

"Justified? You call slaughtering half a kingdom only because they wanted a small parcel of land justified?"

Thallan snorted. "It was elven territory, and we had the right to defend it."

The man yelled and stomped his foot.

"It was our lives, and you'll pay for it!"

Thallan stumbled backward, and the goblin sneered.

"The elf remains cursed to darkness since there is no light in his cruel heart," he said as he faded from view. Thallan watched him vanish. Then his eyes strayed back to Isa and fastened there.

No light. The goblin was right. There was no light in his heart. His light was there—in that small, weak human girl. She was his light.

The enemy gathered around him, but his gaze did not waver.

"Balin," Ramona whispered, perspiration rolling down her forehead.

Balin immediately went on alert. The bright glow from the cage was beginning to wane. He turned worried eyes to his friend, still trapped, but for how much longer?

Thallan's power shone around him like a blue halo, steadily growing brighter and more prominent, but darkness tainted the light— violent darkness. It thrashed about wildly as if screaming and raging at its diminishing control while the warrior stood utterly still, staring blankly into space. What did he see?

Ramona gasped a second before the cage shattered. The impact of it blasted her and Balin a few feet away. But Thallan remained frozen. Ramona didn't dare take her eyes off him. Not while the black streams of evil remained. The fierce battle continued to rage, the blue light of his power, his very will, struggling against the all-consuming darkness of the curse. Both fighting for control.

His blue aura pulsed with each breath he took, pushing back against the encroaching darkness. The struggle intensified until, finally, his power prevailed. The blackness the goblin had placed in him faded and sank back through his skin, leaving only the soft blue glow surrounding him.

Ramona exhaled sharply when Thallan's eyes returned to their natural color, the silver ring slowly fading. Thallan stared at both of them, the torment and guilt written plainly on his face as realization dawned. It was the last thing they saw before he turned and vanished into the trees.

Ramona's shoulders shook as she fell to the ground sobbing. Balin picked her up and walked slowly back towards the house. Ramona was asleep before he reached their quarters. Gently, he laid her on the bed and stroked her hair away from her face. Even in rest, she looked worried. Such was the price they paid for their loyalty.

Sunlight beamed through the open window, rousing Isa. She groaned as she sat up and grabbed her head, where a headache was quickly forming. She hadn't realized she'd injured that, too, yesterday.

She turned bleary eyes to her surroundings. The rustic walls of her small cottage bedroom told her she hadn't been having a nightmare. Thallan had almost killed her. Balin had saved her, and Ramona had rushed to protect him.

Ignoring the protest from her body, Isa jumped off the bed and hurried to the door, throwing it wide open. The silence was deafening. She rushed to the kitchen to find the female elf. Surely, she had awakened by now. But only emptiness greeted her there. Beginning to panic, Isa ran to Ramona's bedroom. There she found them, Balin sitting by the bed and Ramona lying under the covers, still and pale as death.

Lord Alistair paced the floors, hands behind his back.

"My Lord."

He turned sharply and grasped the guard by his shirt. "Where is she?" he asked, shaking the man.

The guard swallowed nervously. "She is yet to be found, My Lord," he answered.

"Useless," Lord Alistair stated impatiently, shoving him aside. He stalked out of the room, bumping into someone in the hall.

"My Lord," Princess Nixa breathed, barely catching herself from falling.

Lord Alistair gave her a distracted bow, not really seeing her.

"Your Highness."

He continued promptly on his way without waiting for a response.

"Wait," she said, grabbing his arm.

He could barely restrain himself from tossing her aside as he had done his guard.

"Yes, Princess?" he said through gritted teeth.

"Where are you going? I was just on my way to see you." She stroked his arm flirtatiously.

Lord Alistair watched her slender fingers trail over his bicep, then gripped them none too gently. He gave her an icy look that could freeze lava and stormed off. Nixa watched him go, her eyes narrowing to slits. Even in death, Lady Isabella was a thorn in her flesh.

Chapter 12

Isa turned the page of the book and absent-mindedly scanned the writing. Balin had frowned on her bringing the books to the cottage when they'd left the manor, insisting they only had room for the bare necessities. But Isa refused to back down. She was still determined to find some way to break Thallan's curse.

This book was ancient. She had only read the introduction but could already tell it was promising. She would have to look through it later, though. She had more important things to do now. Laying the book on the couch, she picked her way around the mess in the small living space and went to Ramona and Balin's room.

"Hello," she said, softly opening the door.

Balin turned around to give her a quick glance, then looked back down at his mate. The dark circles under his pale eyes worried her. It had already been over a day since they had fled the manor. It was no longer safe to be around Thallan, and they couldn't stay at the manor without him. Not with Isa's life still in danger.

Balin had refused to sleep since they arrived at their new home, insisting that he would rest after Ramona woke. From the one book she had skimmed through the night before, Isa knew that elves could function a long time without sleep, but the fight with Thallan had taken a toll on him. Sighing, she walked to Ramona's bedside and found her resting peacefully. Her chest rose and fell gently, and Isa felt a sense of relief wash over her. At least her elven friend was safe, for now.

"Has she woken up at all?" Isa whispered, turning her attention back to Balin.

The man tiredly shook his head.

"No, she hasn't. But she's stable, so that's a good sign."

Isa frowned, guilt rising within her. She knew what had happened was the result of Thallan's curse, but she couldn't help but feel that she was somehow responsible as well.

"I'm sorry," she said softly.

"It's not your fault," Balin replied, his gaze still on his mate. "The curse would eventually have taken him to this extreme, with or without your presence."

Isa nodded and left him to his solitary vigil. The love and anxiety radiating from the elf was too much for her to bear. Clearly, the devotion he and Ramona shared was deep. Isa's heart ached. It was the kind of love she had always dreamed of but had never experienced. One she feared she never would experience.

An image of Thallan sprang to mind. She might could have had it, but things had gone so terribly wrong. If only she could break his curse and free him from these violent compulsions. But how?

She trudged to the kitchen and busied herself making a simple meal. Ramona had taught her a few things during her stay at the manor, and she felt thankful that she could at least keep them from starving, not that Balin would eat much, if anything, while Ramona slept.

While she went through the motions of preparing the food, Isa's mind wandered back to what she had read that morning. The kettle she'd put on the stove for tea started boiling. Distracted by her thoughts, she grabbed it to put in the tea leaves. She tore her hand away when the hot metal burned her, plunging it into a bowl of cold water.

Memories of the night Thallan had cleaned her wounds rose to her mind, and she wondered what he was doing now. Was he okay? Had he succumbed to the curse, or was he still fighting it?

After a few moments, when the sharp pain had morphed into a dull throb, she removed her hand and got back to work. Once everything was ready, she lifted the heavy tray and carried it to Ramona's room. Maybe she could get Balin to eat something. She would try.

The kitchen fell silent upon her departure, and Thallan stepped out of the shadows. His gaze lingered on the kettle, and his eyes watered. At least she lived. When he'd seen Isa in his vision of the battlefield amongst his other victims, he'd thought he'd killed her. He *had* almost killed her. The realization nearly paralyzed him.

Soon.

He would make sure she was safe. Then, he would rid the world of the terror of his presence. His spirit was broken, his proud shoulders slumped. He stepped back into the comfort of the shadows.

"The death toll keeps rising. The people are uneasy, and nobody feels safe anymore."

The king stared at his Prime Minister. "I am well aware," he said. "In this very castle, a member of the court was taken a few weeks ago. All efforts to find her have been fruitless."

The Lord Chamberlain nodded in agreement, "Indeed, Your Majesty, Lady Isabella, daughter of the former Prime Minister. A thorough search of her room revealed that she took no personal belongings. No clothing or toiletries that is, but her maid said that her jewels and purse were missing. However, there were no signs of forced entry or even a struggle. It's as if she just vanished into thin air."

"So, it was someone she knew? Someone she would leave with willingly?" asked one of the nobles. "Her confession letter that the princess found did mention that she was running off with someone."

"But if she ran away with someone, she would have taken her clothes and personal items," insisted another noble. "At least one dress. As it is, no clothes are missing. She would've had to have left in her nightgown."

"Maybe she planned on buying more."

"That doesn't make sense. Why would she buy more when it would be so easy to grab some of what she had? She couldn't have been in much of a hurry if she had time to take her jewels that were shut away in her vanity."

"Perhaps whoever took her forced her to tell him where she kept her valuables, and then he took them," suggested another noble.

"If someone had kidnapped her, surely there would have been some sign of struggle."

"The letter the princess found specifically said that she'd run away. Whatever her reasons, it seems clear that no foul play was involved," insisted the first noble.

"Someone could have faked that letter," suggested the second. All eyes shot to the king. After all, hinting that his daughter might have done something so treacherous was dangerous, and if anyone had done it, the most likely suspect *was* the princess.

The king pursed his lips and stared off into the distance. "It's possible that someone could have planted that letter in my daughter's quarters." That was all he would concede. Though, he'd had suspicions himself when the paper had first come to light.

The nobles shifted nervously in their seats.

"I got reports that a few days before her disappearance, someone killed Lord Byron and his entire guard right in his home," the guard captain said. "And it's grown increasingly worse. We've always had murders in the city. People die all the time, but recently it's grown much worse."

"So, do we think the lady's disappearance and the surge of murders are connected?" asked the Prime Minister.

"How could they be?" asked the first noble. "She wasn't killed. She just disappeared. I still think she ran away as the letter said."

"The people who have died in these attacks," said the king, "are they all men, or are some women?"

"They are all men, Your Majesty," replied the captain.

"Is that significant?" asked the Prime Minister.

"Maybe. I'm not sure. Who were they? Wealthy men, poor men, influential?"

"Other than Lord Byron, there were a few minor nobles and their guards, a few wealthy merchants and their guards, a guild president, the main witness for an upcoming trial, some major landowners, and people like that."

"No regular, unimportant people?"

"No, Your Majesty."

"What are you thinking?" asked the Lord Chamberlain.

"It sounds like everyone who has been a part of this murder spree was someone of importance, at least, of importance to somebody. They sound like people who others might want dead for various reasons."

"A hired assassin?" asked the captain.

The nobles all glanced around the room, studying each other's faces. Who among them might have contacted an assassin?

"That might explain the situation with Lady Isabella," suggested the Lord Chamberlain.

"How so?" asked the Prime Minister.

"She is a lady of importance, an heiress, in fact, and a beautiful one at that. It's possible that someone would want her dead."

A few nervous eyes shifted to the king, only to dart away again. Everyone knew of the animosity between the lady in question and the princess.

The king froze in his seat, his eyes sharp and his expression hard.

"So, you're saying someone hired an assassin to kill her as well?" asked the Prime Minister.

The Lord Chamberlain shrugged. "Perhaps."

"Then why didn't we find her body like we found the bodies of the others?"

"Maybe he changed his mind."

The Prime Minister's eyes widened in disbelief. "Changed his mind?" He looked around at the others and scoffed.

"None of the other victims were women," explained the Lord Chamberlain. "And Lady Isabella is quite lovely. Perhaps," he insisted, "he decided not to go through with it after he saw her."

"And what? He kidnapped her instead?"

"It would explain things: why she didn't take any personal possessions, why there was no sign of struggle. An assassin would be a professional, after all. He would be able to discharge his duties efficiently."

"And the purse and jewels?"

"Maybe he forced her to tell him where they were and grabbed them before he left. Maybe he came back for them later. Who knows, but it is possible."

"And the letter?"

"I don't believe the letter," admitted the Lord Chamberlain. I think it was forged as an afterthought when the lady's body never appeared."

The Prime Minister huffed. "That's a great deal of speculation."

"Without much evidence, speculation is almost all we have right now," he insisted.

The king held up his hand for silence. "We will remove the copies of that letter that are posted throughout the kingdom."

The Prime Minister started to argue, but the king gave him a stern look, and he backed down.

"The copies have been up long enough to punish the lady if the information in them is true; however, now that some doubt has been raised about their authenticity, it would be better to remove them before more harm can be done. In the meantime, we will investigate this idea of an assassin more thoroughly." The king turned to the guard captain. "Have your men question all of their contacts who are even remotely connected in that area."

The guard captain cleared his throat and glanced around nervously. "Even the royal problem-fixer?"

"Especially, the royal problem-fixer. We all need things taken care of occasionally, but this has gotten out of hand. The situation must be contained and brought back under our control."

"As you wish, your majesty."

The other nobles mumbled amongst themselves as the king rose and left the room.

Ramona groaned as she stirred.

"My love!" Balin exclaimed, grasping her hand tighter. She opened her eyes slowly and saw his worried face bent over hers.

"Balin, my love, you don't have to hover so," she said with a laugh as she sat up. "I'm perfectly fine."

Balin eyed her suspiciously before he relaxed. "It took four days this time. It was only two the time before. It's costing you more each time," he said to her.

Ramona squeezed his hands lovingly. "A sacrifice I'm willing to make. Besides...," she said, swinging her feet off the bed, "I have a strong feeling I won't have to do it again."

At that moment, Isa knocked on the door. She opened it a crack and looked in, only to see them staring back at her. She smiled on seeing Ramona sitting up and rushed into the room.

"And this is the reason for my strong feeling," Ramona said, hugging her friend.

"I feared you wouldn't recover. You looked so pale. I mean, you still look pale now, but you looked even paler before. Balin said you would be alright, and I know you are an elf and all that, but you still had me worried."

Ramona patted Isa's back lightly and laughed. "It's going to take more than making a little light cage to get rid of one of the most experienced light elves around."

Isa wiped her tears. "That means you are a descendant of Caladon," she said, grinning widely.

Ramona raised a brow. "I see someone has been brushing up on elven history."

Isa shrugged. "More like I sneezed my way through the old, dusty book, but yes, I was curious."

Balin quietly left the room. Isa could take care of Ramona now that she'd recovered. It was his turn to rest.

Randellstaff's eyes settled on the bundle Lord Alistair had just placed on the floor. He looked around the room, confused about why it was full of dusty ancient artifacts. They seemed out of place in a bedroom owned by one of the land's wealthiest and most powerful lords.

"What will we need that large piece of equipment for?" He asked.

Alistair just glared at him before continuing to drag his contraption into the closet. A crash sounded from within, followed by complete silence.

Alistair reentered the bedroom. "Mr. Randellstaff, did you ever wonder how my family came into prominence?"

"Never been one to worry about problems I didn't have to worry about," Randellstaff said, wiping his nose on his sleeve.

"Problems," Alaistair said. "Yes, I suppose you could say our rise to success is based on how we have always handled our problems." He walked over to another one of the antiques and began adjusting its metal arm. "You see, I buy my problems, kill them, or on rare occasions," he looked at Randellstaff, "partner with them."

"I can agree with the first two," said the man as he rubbed the scraggly growth on his chin.

"Times are different now than when my family first got started." Alistair finished fiddling with the machine and turned to his unlikely partner. "That past has fallen into the same category as fairytales." He sat his tool down on a table. "And my family is a large part of the reason elves are little more than fairytales today," Alistair said as he walked over and sat on the edge of the bed.

"Oh, really now, are you trying to tell me that your family took on the perfect, all-superior elves? With what, gold coins? Besides," Randellstaff continued, "elves aren't just fairytales. They still live on the other side of the mountains. At least, that's what I've heard."

"I'm sure some do," agreed Alistair. "What do you think we've been preparing for after all?" he asked, his arm stretched towards the antiques on display. "Why do you think I've partnered with members of the assassins' guild," he waved his hand at Randellstaff, "when it was an assassin who started this whole mess in the first place? But, even though elves still live, they are not nearly as numerous or powerful as they once were. And they do not interfere with us anymore, at least not like they did in the past."

"Wait a minute," said Randellstaff, clearly confused. "I thought we were preparing for a dramatic go at rescuing your lover."

"I will excuse your manners due to your usually vile environment." Alistair spat.

"You do know Lady Isabella is probably dead right?" Randellstaff asked with a malicious grin.

"My Isabella can't be dead. Tonight will bring me one step closer to a forever with her."

"So, let me get this straight. Your man told you an assassin kidnapped her, and you think that assassin is an elf? And you're setting a trap for him here?"

"There's no evidence, but if our intel is right, it's the same assassin that took down Lord Byron. That man left a massacre behind him, and Lord Byron always had the best security. Only someone with extraordinary skill and power could pull off such a thing."

"Someone like an elf?"

Alistair glared at the incredulous look on Randellstaff's face. He would believe him eventually. When the villain fell into his trap, Randellstaff would see then that he wasn't crazy.

"So, if the assassin is to blame, why did he take her and not simply kill her as he was hired to do?"

"He was probably charmed by her beauty. Who wouldn't be?"

Randellstaff raised his brows, pursed his lips, and nodded. He'd seen the lady in question before, and he could guess why someone would steal her away instead of killing her, and being charmed didn't have anything to do with it.

"Well," he said, "as long as I see some action, I'll be pleased with the night." He pulled his sword from its scabbard and spun it around excitedly.

"No filthy elf will keep my Isabella away from me. I will die before that happens!" Alistair said in a loud whisper, now on his feet.

"Elf or not, I suppose he'll die just like anyone else." Randellstaff returned his sword to its scabbard and pulled two daggers from his sleeves. Raising them in the air, he threw them across the room. They sliced through a vase by the window, producing a loud crash as the heavy pieces fell to the floor.

"Control yourself, else you'll give the trap away," Alistair commanded.

"You should have thought of that before you put a glowing orb by the window. I had to cover it with a sheet so *it* wouldn't give us away."

Alistair stared in horror as Randellstaff spoke.

"What have you done!"

Alistair rushed past the foolish man, and Randellstaff spun on his heel to watch him. When Alistair got to the covered orb, he threw off the sheet, and a bright green light filled the room.

Randellstaff didn't have even a moment to process the unfolding events before a body dropped from the shadows, falling toward him. He immediately pulled his sword and attacked the bloody mass. The body slumped to the ground, unmoving. A closer look revealed the man was already dead. It was the body of one of his companions who had accompanied him there that night.

He barely had time to react when, out of the corner of his eye, he caught something else flying at him. He jumped out of the way, and the body of his other associate barely missed him as it slammed against the wall. Randellstaff tried to move, but something held him in place. Something gripped his shoulders and spun him around.

A sword plunged into his chest. His weapon fell from his shaking hand as he looked up into light blue eyes ringed by silver. And on each side of the fierce face sat a pointed ear. He felt himself hoisted off the ground, and the last image he saw was Lord Alistair disappearing into the closet. *An elf,* he thought as he struggled to inhale his final breath. *At least, that's an exciting way to die.*

Thallan usually didn't kill unless he received a contract for someone; however, his contact had informed him that this lord had been searching for information on him for quite some time. He'd been inquiring everywhere and speaking to everyone. Something needed to be done before Thallan was exposed. His contact had even suggested that the situation might have something to do with Lady Isabella.

The timing couldn't have been better. Thallan's curse had hardly let up since he'd fulfilled his last contract the night before. He'd even gone out during the day to a public execution in the town square and risked being seen by hundreds of spectators just to shoot an arrow into a man who was about to be hung.

Shadows weren't as deep during the day, and he'd had to take the shot from the rooftops to escape without being seen. But killing was killing, after all, and that had appeased the curse for a little while. However, now, only hours later, it plagued him again. He would have to execute his plan soon, but he wanted to ensure Isa was safe before he went.

From his position on the roof, Thallan could hear them. Four hearts beat in the room below, and one had to be Lord Alistair, his target. He hadn't bothered to take care of the security guards first. He didn't expect this to last long.

Besides, he could always take them out later if the need arose. He just wanted to get this over with as quickly as he could and get back to check on Isa. And Ramona and Balin, of course.

Thallan's mind wandered back to the little cottage where they now stayed, but the sound of a name from a conversation he wasn't paying attention to brought him back to the present moment. He listened more closely, and sure enough, there it was again. "My Isabella can't be dead. Tonight will bring me one step closer to a forever with her."

Not if he had anything to say about it.

Thallan summoned water droplets from the air and gathered them into a platform. He stepped onto it and slowly lowered it until he hovered outside the open window where he could better focus on their conversation.

"No filthy elf will keep my Isa away from me. I will die before that happens!"

That sounded like a challenge to Thallan. He quietly swung in the window and dispatched the heartbeat hidden behind the curtains, obviously a part of some trap. With a hand over the man's mouth and a dagger through his neck, that part of the trap was taken care of. Thallan held the body still and continued to listen from his hiding place. He wanted to see if they said anything more about Isa before he made another move.

"Should have thought of that before you put a glowing orb by the window. I had to cover it with a sheet so it wouldn't do just that, give us away."

Thallan paid attention to the items in the room for the first time since he entered. For some reason, the scattering of antiques made him uneasy. He had nothing to fear from these humans, he reassured himself. Even if they knew what he was, what could they do against the most powerful warrior of the most powerful race?

The green glow from the orb suddenly lit up the room as Alistair removed the sheet. Thallan recognized that glow even before he saw the orb—an elf siren.

He hadn't seen one since the war. He certainly wasn't expecting to see one here. The mage craft called to him. It was designed to calm the elven mind, to lull it into numbness and complacency. But Thallan's curse was too strong to be so easily cowed. It revolted against the magic, triggering his troubled thoughts, and vivid memories of the battlefield rushed back. He released his hold on the man's corpse, and it dropped from behind the curtains.

Thallan stepped out of his hiding place and quickly surveyed the space. It was a human nobleman's bedroom, but the familiar battlefield that had troubled Thallan's dreams for so long had somehow morphed onto it. He saw both, the oversized bed and the rocks covered in bodies and dripping with blood.

Moving instinctively, he charged at the nearest enemy warrior and quickly dispatched him. He found himself carried through the motions of battle like a passenger in his own enraged body. He saw another enemy try to get away and launched himself after him.

That opponent was also easily disposed of. Suddenly, a sharp pain shot through his right shoulder. He glanced at the injury only to find what appeared to be a snakehead at the end of a chain, gripping his shoulder blade in a powerful bite. What was more surprising was that the snakehead and the chain that held it appeared to be made of light, light that had burned right through his flesh.

Alistair had known that all might be lost as soon as he saw the bright green glow of the orb. It was supposed to shine faintly when an elf was nearby. How brightly it glowed depended on how close and how powerful the elf was. His shone with a blinding light.

His only hope lay in the closet, and he dashed for it. In the few steps it took him to reach the small room, he heard chaos erupt behind him. He didn't bother to check if anyone was still alive.

He unsheathed his dagger as he went through the door. He had to fill the activation chamber of the anti-elf contraption with blood to make it work, if it worked.

The small silver canon perched on its eight legs in the middle of his hanging clothes. The activation chamber sat on the top of the device like the head on a spider. Alistair heard a loud crash behind him just as he reached the machine. He quickly cut his hand and held it over the chamber. The machine lit up when his dripping blood landed on the crystal inside.

Alistair backed away from the device just as a white chain made of light shot out from one of the glowing cannon legs. With his blood powering it, the chamber spun atop the center of the cannon, and as it turned, the other legs also began to glow. His eyes followed the second chain as it shot out, and widened when he spotted its target.

A tall elf stood where the wall had been moments earlier. His long silver hair swirled around his shoulders wildly, propelled by the aura of his magic. His piercing blue eyes, surrounded by silver rings, froze Alistair in place with their cold, cruel glare. He radiated violence and death. Alistair only just stopped himself from wetting his pants. As it was, his terror held him immobile.

So, this was an elf, he thought. How did any of his ancestors stand a chance against their kind? He could only watch and hope his machine took down this terrible threat. He knew there was no way he would survive this encounter if it didn't.

The scream that erupted from Thallan's throat pierced the air as the serpent heads of light bit into his flesh. Each leg of the machine shot out its projectile, and when they had all pierced their target, they began dragging the elf toward the room and the deadly contraption it held.

When the seventh head had torn through Thallan's hand after he tried catching it, he knew he had to get out of there fast. The eighth chain hit him on his temple, and immediately, he felt his strength begin to leave his body as the chains dragged him toward the machine. The pressure in his head from the curse had left him at the first stab of pain, and he could think clearly now.

How did a human have an ancient weapon from the War of the Species? Thallan recognized it, and when he saw the main head spinning, he knew he was in trouble. His strength was almost gone. He would only have one chance.

Thallan closed his eyes and focused inward. Somehow, he found the energy and summoned all the magic he had left. With a final effort, he aimed it at the activation chamber.

The blood in it shifted toward him. The motion threw the sensitive contraption off center, and the machine started to howl violently and rock back and forth. One of the legs snapped in two. It was the one whose light held Thallan by his temple, and he immediately felt some of his strength return when that light dissipated.

With a roar, he pulled the blood toward himself, ripping it from the magical chamber. The machine exploded, throwing debris everywhere. Still weakened, Thallan saw his chance to escape and took it before the human activated another anti-elf device.

Chapter 13

The Alistair estate was abuzz with activity as the sun began to rise. Everyone had heard the fight. It would have been impossible not to. But the action had happened so quickly that it was already over before Alistair's guards managed to break down the door and get to him. Soldiers and mercenaries of all kinds littered the compound now, but Lord Alistair, alone, was in his damaged bedroom where the attack had taken place.

He walked through the debris as soon as he'd recovered enough to move. The lord snorted as he glanced down at the bodies of Randellstaff and his men. He was supposed to be one of the best bodyguards money could buy.

"He had his uses," Alistair said, pushing the corpse out of his way with his foot.

Now that he had confirmation that his adversary was indeed an elf and that the ancestral weapons stored in his family vault worked, he saw this situation in a whole new light. The device he had just used was the first of many. His family had collected an arsenal all those centuries ago. One day, he would go through every weapon he had and see how it could best be used to further his political prospects. His mind raced at the possibilities, but not now.

He needed to go after his elven attacker while the trail was still fresh and the mythical beast was wounded. The last encounter had taught him he couldn't be over-prepared to face a creature like that. So, he quickly examined the most powerful-looking devices, trying to decide which would be best to take with him in his pursuit.

At this point, Alistair had to ask himself if Isabella was still his goal. He remained determined to get her back, but now it felt like destiny also drove him to a higher purpose. He needed to go after that demon. He needed to rid the world of their kind.

He picked up a heavy gauntlet that bore a label reading "Heart in Hand." *That doesn't sound very combative*, he thought as he put it on and pulled the straps to tighten it. He felt a rush of excitement as it powered up.

A sharp pain pierced his hand as needles stabbed his wrist. He grimaced but didn't remove the device. The cannon had required blood as well. He would just have to bear this if he wanted to use these weapons.

His blood slickened his hand inside the gauntlet. He tried to adjust it to release some of the pressure, but it wouldn't budge. Instead, it resized and reshaped itself, fitting more snuggly and comfortably, all the while letting off a gentle hum.

Excited, Alistair decided to test his new weapon. After all, he would need to know how to work it before he met the elf again. He looked around until he spotted a lone mercenary sitting in the courtyard. Hiding behind the wall, Alistair peeked out the bedroom window into the yard and extended his left arm, aiming the gauntlet at the mercenary.

The glove began to pulse slowly, then gradually faster and more intensely. He instinctively contracted his fingers, and a red, messy mass appeared to slam into his hand. Alistair stared at it. The pulsing of the gauntlet was in sync with that of the bloody blob he now held. Realization struck him suddenly. It was a heartbeat. He raised his head to see the mercenary slumped over on the ground with a bloodied chest.

Lord Alistair smiled at the gradually slowing beat of the heart. This was the perfect weapon for an elf who had stolen the woman he loved.

Balin leaned against a tree, watching the manor as the sun rose. Thallan had been gone a long time this night, but that wasn't surprising. Balin knew better than to follow him into town or to even make his presence known, but he couldn't abandon his friend completely. He still felt the need to check on him now and again. So, he stood there, waiting patiently for his return.

He noticed a noise in the trees off in the distance but ignored it. It would be some animal. Thallan didn't make noise when he moved through the forest. But then he heard it again, and something about the sound grabbed his attention. It almost sounded like shuffling footsteps.

Balin was instantly off to check it out and soon came across a blood trail. A thud behind him immediately drew his eyes. Thallan lay in a bloody black and red heap on the forest floor. After checking his injuries, Balin picked up his friend and hurried back to the manor.

Back in the cottage, Ramona sensed through their blood bond that something was wrong. She grabbed Isa, and the two set off for the manor.

Thallan woke slowly, whispers in familiar voices pulling him back to consciousness.

"Isn't he supposed to have super elf healing powers or something?"

"I don't know why his healing hasn't kicked in. Mine hasn't worked on him either." Ramona frantically waved her hands over his bloody wounds. They didn't close as they should have. "These injuries are different. They look like magic burn bites of some sort that went straight through his flesh and into bone. I might be able to counter them, but it will take time."

"Let her go," Thallan spoke up in a hollow voice.

"What?" Ramona asked, struggling to hear him.

Thallan grabbed Ramona's arm. Balin jumped into a defensive stance, but Ramona stopped him with a gesture.

"Let Isa go. They are coming." A rough cough interrupted him. But he soon caught his breath. "See that she's safe." With those words, he fell back onto the pillow, his eyes closing once again.

"Yes, Your Highness," Ramona mumbled.

"Wait, what? Your Highness?" Isa stared down at the bloody elf in surprise.

Ramona rose from her seat on the bed and began washing her hands, and Balin immediately took her spot.

"I'm right here, Thallan. Who is coming?" Isa asked frantically. But Thallan didn't respond.

Ramona turned to Isa.

"Let's go," she said calmly.

"What?" Isa seemed confused.

"You heard my orders. I'm to escort you to safety."

Isa opened her mouth to protest, "But..."

"But nothing, Isa, whoever or whatever put the prince in this state is on their way here, and I guarantee you don't want to be here when they arrive."

Isa stood motionless, staring at Thallan. "The prince?" She shook her head. She had to concentrate on what was important. She'd think about that later. "I can't leave him," she said, "not like this."

"Be reasonable, Isa. How can we face whatever did that to him while trying to protect you at the same time? It will be difficult enough as it is."

"Maybe I can help," Isa replied weakly.

Ramona just stared at her with raised brows. "Let me carry out my orders." She extended a hand, and Isa reluctantly took it.

Lord Alistair led his soldiers and as many mercenaries as his gold could buy through the forest. The chill of the air sank into his bones, and the thrill of his excitement began to wane. They'd been searching the woods for hours, and even though they periodically spotted drops of blood, the elf's trail was proving frustratingly difficult to follow.

Alistair touched his left hand through his cloak with his right. He felt the comforting warmth of the gauntlet, and a renewed sense of purpose gave him the energy he needed to continue. He motioned for his soldiers to increase their pace. He had enough men. They would search the whole forest if they had to.

After what seemed like an eternity, a scout eventually spotted the old, crumbling manor. With one glance at its poor state, Alistair almost signaled to move on, but then he saw the blood trail. It was the clearest one they'd come across yet. He motioned for the men to stop. He sent a few up to the building to see what they could find. The others would rest.

He hoped his prey was so wounded that he wouldn't put up much of a fight, but Alistair didn't want to take any chances. Besides, there might be other elves in there. They would need to be ready to face whatever awaited them.

The scouts returned with a less-than-helpful report. Someone was there, but they couldn't discover who. They'd seen a light on an upper floor, but it was impossible to know anything else unless they entered the building. The structure was too damaged to climb. Did he want them to try to find a way in?

Alistair's impatience had grown steadily as he waited for the men to return. Wisdom dictated that he gather more information before he made a move, but he didn't want to wait. The desire to kill an elf—to be the first human in years who had managed to do so—overwhelmed him. And every second, the creature's magic healing powers could be undoing the damage he had already managed to inflict. Several hours had already passed since their last encounter. He feared to face the elf after he had healed, even with the multitude of men he had surrounding him.

That fear was just the push that he needed to ignore wisdom and give the order to advance. As the men moved forward, the front door creaked slightly ajar, and Isa started to emerge. She was quickly pulled back into the house. At the sight of the girl's retreat, Alistair revealed his gauntlet and yelled.

"Attack!" he ordered as he charged towards the entrance.

Just before Ramona pulled her back in, Isa had caught a glimpse of the force outside.

"It's Lord Alistair," she said.

Ramona barricaded the door with a spell and turned to face the girl.

"Who?"

"Lord Alistair. I think they might be here for me."

Something heavy crashed into the door, and it vibrated from the impact, but Ramona's barricade held.

"Make the choice now," she said. "Prince Thallan has freed you, not that you ever were a prisoner," she added as an afterthought. "These men *might* be here for you, so you probably won't be harmed, but they are *definitely* here to kill the prince. And I don't know how, but they almost succeeded the first time. So I can't go with you. If you leave now, you should be safe.

Go out the library windows. I'll keep them occupied here, just in case."

Isabella hesitated for only a moment. "Come on, we need to get to Balin so you both can prepare our defenses."

"*Our* defenses?"

"Yes, *our* defenses. You and he are both needed to hold them off, and the least I can do is watch over Thallan, especially since this feels like my fault."

"You're lucky there's no time for any further discussion," Ramona said as they ran back to the bedroom.

Isabella anxiously squeezed Thallan's hand, her eyes glued to the doorway. Her elf lay unconscious, only occasionally mumbling something incoherently. They'd heard the crash when the men broke through the main door. They could track their progress through the mansion by the noise of the destruction they left behind.

Shouts heralded their arrival outside the bedroom door, and the trio prepared themselves for the fight. The men battered at the wood for several minutes, but Ramona's light shield held firm. She and Balin stood directly behind it, ready to defend them all if need be.

Strong as her shield was, it couldn't hold forever against such force. The door finally burst open with a resounding crash. Isa jumped as Balin and Ramona were flung back. But Balin didn't hit the floor like Ramona did. His body floated off the ground as if by magic, and he gripped his chest tightly as he was pulled toward the door.

Lord Alistair entered the room, gauntlet first, with his left arm stretched towards the male elf. Ramon lifted her hand and created a light shield around her mate. Balin fell to the ground when the shield activated, the gauntlet losing its hold.

Alistair turned to Ramona, and the gauntlet reactivated on her. "Your elf hearts seem a bit more difficult to extract than those of humans," he said, "and your powers might temporarily block it. But don't be deceived. I will be victorious here." Alistair winced as the gauntlet drew more blood but kept his hand outstretched.

Ramona had no choice but to place and hold a second shield around herself. Her powers were beginning to weaken, though. She still hadn't fully recovered from her fight with Thallan. Shielding the doors and both of them was starting to take its toll. Balin pushed himself to his feet and started to go to his mate.

"No," said Ramona, the strain in her voice evident. "Don't move. I can hold them both as long as you stay still."

Balin frowned, but he nodded. However, he rested his hand his sword and got into a battle stance. If Ramona's barrier failed, he would be ready.

The rest of Alistair's company spilled into the room, their weapons drawn. They quickly took in the strange scene, unsure whether or not they should interfere. So, they stood by, waiting for orders.

"The most amazing thing I noticed about this gauntlet," Alistair said conversationally, ignoring his men. He'd relaxed considerably now that it was evident he had the upper hand. "Is that once a heart is requested, the gauntlet locks in on the target and will continue pulling at it for as long as I wish." He smirked at Balin and Ramona, enjoying their desperate situation.

Satisfied that those elves posed no danger, he turned to Isa. His lip curled in distaste when he realized she sat on the bed beside the male elf he had come to kill.

"My darling Isabella," he said with a slight bow, still holding the gauntlet out in front of him. "I've come to rescue you."

"Then stop this attack at once! I'm not a captive here. These are my friends." Isa pleaded with him. "Thallan saved my life!"

Alistair winced again as the gauntlet drew more blood, and that's when he noticed that Isa held the elf's hand.

"My Lady, why are you still pretending to care for him? I have the power over these vile creatures, and I'm here to rescue you. Release him and come with me." Alistair held his other hand out to Isa, his voice now racked with pain.

"I'm not pretending, Lord Alistair. Please, I just want the bloodshed to end."

Alistair suddenly started shaking his head and hitting it with his right hand.

"No, no, no, he's brainwashed you. Can't you see?" he insisted desperately.

The gauntlet's power increased as it sucked out more blood. He fell to one knee in pain. Ramona strained under the weapon's increased effect and barely managed to keep herself and Balin from flying across the room.

"Alistair, stop this. It's killing you," Isa yelled.

Alistair took several deep breaths and struggled get back to his feet. His gaze bypassed Isa and focused on Thallan.

"I'll gladly give myself to end that monster!" He screamed and turned the gauntlet on Thallan.

The gauntlet hummed more loudly as it pulled additional blood from its source. Alistair grunted and reached up to grab it with his other hand, holding on tightly. Ramona's powers were stretched to their limit. She couldn't protect Thallan, too. Isa recognized this and immediately threw herself between her elf and the gauntlet.

"So be it, Isabella. So be it!" screamed Alistair hysterically.

A soft blue light shrouded Thallan's body at that instant. He moved so quickly that he seemed to vanish from the bed and reappear in front of her. The magic of the gauntlet hit him full force. He growled before falling to one knee.

Alistair's shrill laughter pierced the air, causing his men to glance at him askance. He sounded like a madman. Many of the mercenaries recognized how unhinged he had become and decided that wasn't a wise place to be. They quietly retreated from the room and fled the manor.

Thallan knelt, bent over with his head bowed. He protected his heart with one hand while slowly lifting the other in the air.

"You will not survive this time, you filthy..." the rest of the words died in Alistair's throat.

He stood with his arm still stretched out in front of him, but when he looked down at the sudden sting of pain, he saw only empty space where his hand, and the gauntlet, had been. He watched in shock as blood squirted out of his arm where his hand had been ripped away. He let out a piercing scream and fell to his knees.

"The human body contains water, and water is my faithful servant," said Thallan weakly.

The gauntlet, still enclosing Alistair's severed hand and gushing blood, hovered in the air close to Thallan's outstretched arm. It slowly turned, now facing the intruders. The remaining soldiers and mercenaries began dropping like flies as their beating hearts flew out of their chests to float in the air alongside the gauntlet.

Everything fell to the ground when Thallan lowered his hand, and with a sigh of relief, he sagged to the floor. Suddenly, the gauntlet hummed loudly again and flew into Thallan's chest, attempting to bore into his skin. Alistair laughed, less and less blood pouring from his bloody stump as he bled out.

"I told you, once a heart is requested, the gauntlet does not stop until the request is revoked. And I will *never* revoke it. Don't feel so bad, elf. This is a much kinder fate for your heart than what that woman would have done with it."

Alistair gave a final laugh before he crumbled to the floor. Ramona collapsed in exhaustion as her shields dissipated, and Balin instantly pulled her into his arms. Isa rushed to Thallan and knelt beside him, unsure of how to help. The gauntlet had managed to pierce his flesh and was digging in deeper by the second.

It was an odd sensation, thought Thallan, this gauntlet in his chest. Even though he couldn't yet feel the metal of its fingers around his heart, he could feel the magic surrounding it. It squeezed so tightly, pressing harder with every passing moment. It was crushing it. Thallan grabbed the glove with both hands and tried to pull it out.

"Die!"

He opened his eyes and looked around. Usually, his visions wanted him to kill. This was a different command.

A new specter had joined the group that constantly tormented him. Alistair floated there now, holding onto the gauntlet with his remaining hand as if, even in death, he was still determined to crush the elf's heart.

Perhaps this is for the best, thought Thallan. Ramona and Balin would care for Isa, and he would no longer be a danger to the world. He would have to die soon anyway. It would be safer for everyone if it happened now.

He loosened his hold on the gauntlet. It bore deeper into his body until the metal finally reached his rapidly beating heart. Thallan gasped in pain as the glove tightly squeezed the weakening organ.

Yes. It was time to let go. He closed his eyes and fell to the floor. As he landed, he felt the pressure on his heart decrease. So, this was the peace of death.

"Don't you dare die on me, you stubborn elf!" Isa screamed.

Thallan weakly opened his eyes to see his beloved human bending over him with her hand buried in his chest. No, not her hand. She was wearing the gauntlet. He turned his face to the side and saw Alistair's dismembered appendage lying on the floor beside her.

Understanding pierced his clouded mind. She had removed the dead hand and now wielded the gauntlet herself. He winced as he felt her pull it out of his chest.

"If anyone is going to have your heart, it's me," she said as she threw the gauntlet on the floor. Thallan glanced around. The vision of Alistair hovered in the back of the room behind his other victims. Without his dead hand in the magical glove, he had lost his power.

"After all," continued Isa, staring down at Thallan, "it only seems fair that the fate of your heart belongs to me since you're the one who kidnapped *my* heart."

Thallan's eyes shot back to the girl. "I kidnapped you that night, not your heart,"

"Who said I'm talking about the same night?" she smirked.

A spark of hope burst forth in Thallan, only to be quickly quashed. Isa was caught up in the emotion of the situation. Adrenaline would do that to a person. But this was as good a time as any to let her know how he felt. He wanted her to know, before he ended it all.

"My heart is as much in your hands now as it was a few moments ago. Do with it what you will."

Isa beamed. Her smile could only be matched by that of Ramona sitting with Balin behind them.

"For now," said Isa, rubbing Thallan's bloody but slowly healing chest, "keep it safe for me here."

Thallan grabbed her hand. "I love you. I want you to know that." He stared into her face, his eyes locked onto hers. "You are kind and brave and smart and generous." He reached up and stroked her cheek. "You are the sunshine that broke through the darkness of my existence. You are the air that breathed life into my stagnant world. Don't ever forget how special you are."

"You didn't say beautiful," replied Isa with a soft, breathy laugh.

Thallan smiled. "You are so incredibly beautiful, and while that makes you even more desirable, that isn't what makes you special. You are special because you are you. And I love you so much." He poured all of the longing and sorrow of their upcoming separation into that statement. Isa must have noticed. Confusion covered her face.

"You sound like you're saying 'goodbye.'"

"I have to leave, Isa. I'm not safe to be around. You know that."

Tears filled her eyes.

"No, Thallan. You can't go. Please don't leave me."

"I have to."

"No. That's not fair. I love you. You can't leave me now." Isa threw herself against him. She wrapped her arms tightly, possessively, around his neck and kissed him with all the passion of her desperate soul.

As her lips melted against his, a warmth and lightness spread from his heart throughout his whole body as if the weight of a thousand worlds had been lifted away. He didn't need to be told the curse was gone, but his suspicions were confirmed when he finally opened his eyes and saw that the visions of his victims no longer floated around him. Isa had finally found a way to set him free.

Thallan felt born anew as he rode past the magical boundary into the elven lands. He was finally home. He couldn't wait to show Isa his kingdom. True, she was human, and the elves didn't like humans, but since she had broken his curse and saved his life at significant risk to her own, he had no doubt that his people would accept her. Once they wed and had completed the blood bond, she would share his lifespan, and they could be together forever.

He smiled down at the beauty beside him. "Welcome to Caelora."

Isa had no regrets. There was no other place that she would rather be than here with her elf assassin. She smiled as she rode with Thallan into their new world.

The End

Note from the Author

Thank you for taking the time to read one of my books! I'm enjoying writing this series. I've had a love for fairytales ever since I was a child, and I've long enjoyed reading retellings of "Beauty and the Beast," so I decided to write one of my own. It's been tremendous fun.

It would just thrill me to pieces if you would leave a review of this book on Goodreads or your favorite bookstore's website. I enjoy reading them. It makes me feel just a little bit more connected to all of you out there who share my love of reading and love of fantasy. Thanks in advance.

Turn the page for an excerpt from Book 2 in the series—Cursing Beauty. I hope you enjoy it.

Chapter 1

Girls glow green when you cursed them. At least, that's what he'd been told. He was about to discover for himself whether that was true or not.

The young elf mage stepped forward from amidst the crowd, his rage burning like an inferno. He had just buried his brother, and the people responsible for his death were celebrating the new life entering their family.

That wasn't fair.

But he could fix it.

He would make it fair. He would make them suffer the same pain he felt. They would soon know the anguish of losing a loved one.

Still, even through the red haze of his fury, he couldn't see the justice of murdering a newborn baby. He would curse her instead. Yes, that would be better, he thought. That way, the king would have years to agonize over the horror that was to come.

All the lords and ladies in attendance had given the baby princess their gifts; now, it was his turn.

As he approached the bassinet, the space seemed to buzz with anticipation. Here was an elf. They were rarely seen on this side of the mountains. It was remarkable, indeed, that one had made the trip to honor their princess.

They didn't understand.

They didn't know.

All eyes were on him, and a hush fell over the crowd.

"My gift to the princess is this," the elf said, looking down at the baby. "On her eighteenth birthday, she will prick her finger on the thorn of a rose and fall into an eternal death-like sleep."

The crowd gasped in horror. The king jumped to his feet, but the elf held up his hand. He wasn't finished.

"Only the kiss of true love can awaken her," he said loudly. The guards that had begun to rush toward him stopped to listen.

"But she will never find it. This curse hereby binds her love within itself. Never will she love another, for to the curse alone is she bound."

The elf muttered some words in elvish as the humans looked on in horror. They couldn't move. It was as if the power of the spell held them frozen. Thorn completed his chant and watched in satisfaction as a green glow surrounded the tiny princess.

He turned to the king. "Your selfish actions caused a war that took my brother's life. Now, in payment for that deed, I have taken your daughter's life. I consider us even." With that, the elf vanished.

The courtyard erupted into chaos. Amidst the commotion, the Queen collapsed to the ground in shock. The king knelt by her side, his attention oscillating between comforting his wife and quelling the turmoil around him.

Guards swarmed the area, searching everywhere for the mage, even though it was clear he had gone. Overwhelming helplessness descended on every heart within their ranks. They felt driven to action. Any action. But there was nothing they could do.

The baby princess seemed to sense the tension and began crying in her bassinet.

The elf mage strode through the forest just outside the elven city of Florinia, his mission accomplished.

Princess Elora twisted her long blonde hair into a knot and pinned it at the base of her neck, her mind swirling with thoughts of her upcoming meeting.

She checked the mirror, looking for any escaping strands. Nothing that might reveal her identity could be visible. Secrecy was paramount in case she was seen by a servant or one of the guards. Word couldn't get back to her parents about what she was doing. They would immediately put a stop to it.

Everything looked good. Elora smudged coal powder on the skin around her eyes so it would better blend in with the black mask she would be wearing. How strange it looked.

She stared at her reflection in the mirror.

It stared back.

Their gazes locked, unblinking.

A dull tingle rose up her face, past her nose, and to her eyes. A knot formed in her throat, and her breath felt heavy in her chest. She watched as a single tear escaped her right eye and slowly made its way down her cheek, leaving a coal trail in its wake.

This was not how a princess should look. And secretly meeting a man in her private garden at night was not how a princess should act.

It wasn't fair. Anger toward the elf that had brought her to this state of affairs mingled with anguish at her situation, and a sob tore out of her.

The sound brought her back to the present, and she took a deep breath.

Nope, she thought. *I don't have time to wallow in despair right now. I have more important things to do.*

She would let herself cry as much as she needed to when she returned. If she still felt like it.

Stuffing her emotions into the back of her mind, Elora pulled the black hood up over her head. She rubbed the wayward coal trail off her face and repaired the smudge around her eye. She made one last check in the mirror to make sure her identity was sufficiently concealed.

The black mask hid her eyes and nose, but the hood's shadow barely concealed her mouth. A mouth wasn't terribly recognizable anyway. Was it? Regardless, someone would have to get quite close to her to identify her.

Elora swung her cloak out of the way and climbed over the windowsill. She'd have to be careful coming in and out of her bedroom. The guards couldn't tell who she was, after all. She didn't want to accidentally get shot or stabbed by the very people paid to protect her.

Years ago, she'd asked the gardener to put a trellis outside her bedroom for this very purpose. Not that she'd told him that. He simply believed that she had an obsessive love for honeysuckles. And while she did enjoy their scent, she had no qualms about squashing them when she needed to sneak out of the castle.

Elora quickly climbed down the vine-covered trellis. She'd had a good deal of practice, after all. She had been doing this for years. Ever since she'd first thought of gathering information about the elf who cursed her, her mother and father had forbidden it. They focused on finding someone to break the curse, whether it was another mage or a dashing man.

They claimed that going after the elf, himself, was too dangerous. And maybe it was. They feared him, even though they would never admit it. But she didn't. There wasn't much more he could do to her. Besides, her spies did most of the dangerous work. What could happen to her here in the castle?

Even if the king and queen could be persuaded to target the elf, they certainly would never condone her doing something so rash on her own. And *they* did have more to lose, so she was reduced to this. Sneaking out in the dead of night.

Elora landed lightly and set off across the castle grounds. She had to be quick. She kept to the shadows as she crossed the courtyard, avoiding the torchlight that lined its edges like sentinels.

Elora slipped between the shadows with ease. She moved quickly but silently. She had to duck behind a bush or tree trunk several times as guards walked by, their torches held aloft in their hands like spears in a battle line.

Each time, she silently prayed that they hadn't seen her skulking in the darkness. Finally, after what felt like hours, Elora reached the edge of the palace garden and let out a relieved sigh.

She stepped lightly through the main garden and to the hidden, vine-covered doorway of her personal oasis. She drew her cloak tightly around herself, steeling her resolve as she slipped inside.

Elora scanned the area. The moonlight glinted off the cobblestone path, and the night air was heavy with the scent of more honeysuckles. She really did like how they smelled. Their aroma danced across her nose, and the garden seemed to whisper all around her.

Her heart thudded a little more loudly in her chest, and she could feel each breath she pulled in and pushed out. No matter how often she did this, it never felt any more comfortable.

Exciting. Yes.

But never comfortable.

Isn't that the thing about excitement, though? It rarely goes hand in hand with comfort.

She needn't be quite as cautious here. The guards didn't patrol this place, but still, she stepped lightly. The night was cruel and refused to keep secrets. It would gleefully trumpet any noises, such as the snap of a twig carelessly crushed underfoot, across great distances. Such a thing would send the guards running.

After a few moments of cautious exploration among the flowers and bushes grayed by the moonlight, she spotted her spy. He stood in the center of the garden, his back to her, but as she drew near, he turned.

"I hope you have news for me, Jarden," she said, her voice barely above a whisper.

"I do," he replied gravely. He seemed to hesitate as if weighing his words carefully. "I have just come from the forests outside Allanar. I have a report from our elven spy."

Elora's heart skipped a beat. A wave of anticipation flooded through her. Finding an informant among the elves had been a blessing indeed. "What does he say?"

Jarden took a deep breath. "He says the mage plans to attend a conference in Caelora in two weeks. He should be vulnerable during the trip out."

"Two weeks? That's not much time. We would be pushed to get men in place by then. Do we know when the conference will end? Could we take him on his return journey?"

"Probably not," replied Jarden reluctantly. "He'll most likely use magic to jump back like he did..."

"Like he did when he cursed me," Elora finished for him.

"Yes, Your Highness."

"Are we sure he won't travel to the conference that way?"

"It's doubtful. According to our sources, such travel requires an intimate knowledge of the destination. Without that familiarity, they risk arriving in the wrong place, like inside a tree or rock."

"Ah, yes," said Elora with a snort, "that could be inconvenient for them."

Jarden smirked.

"Where do you think we should intercept him?" she asked. "And how long will it take our men to travel the distance?"

Jarden pulled out a map and spread it over a nearby shrub. Elora could barely read it in the dim light, but it was clear enough for their purposes.

"The safest route through the mountains is Glarendell Pass, provided we don't encounter any goblins. From there, we can ambush him in Evermore

Forest, a few miles from Caelora. We should be able to cover the distance in ten to twelve days, depending on how many men we take. If we don't run into any trouble," he added.

"Well, see if you can get enough men ready to go in time. It would be wonderful if we could capture him then. Since he so rarely leaves Florinia, this might be our only chance before the curse takes hold. We'll stay in touch."

Jarden nodded and turned to go.

Elora waited a few minutes in the garden after the spy had left. She sat back on a bench and breathed in the night air, her earlier trepidation having eased somewhat with her newfound hope.

She would have to make sure everything was set up properly. Now that the basic plan was in place, she could communicate with Jarden via messages. If they were to capture the mage, they would have to do it right, or more of them could end up cursed. Or worse.

Her mind raced with plans, contingencies, and possible outcomes. She couldn't afford to make any mistakes.

As Elora stood to leave, she heard a rustling in the bushes, and her hand went to the dagger she had hidden in her belt. She held her breath, waiting to see if someone would reveal themselves. After a moment of tense silence, a figure stepped out of the foliage.

"Who are you?" she demanded.

The figure moved into the moonlight, revealing himself as a man in his late twenties with dark hair and piercing blue eyes. His tunic and breeches were nondescript, not giving away any information about his societal position. Still, his stance indicated he was a fighter—that and the fact that he comfortably rested his hand on the sword strapped to his waist.

"I am Adrian," he said, bowing his head respectfully. "I heard you talking with your spy. I want to help."

Elora narrowed her eyes suspiciously. "What were you doing in my private garden in the middle of the night?"

"I followed your man here from Allanar."

Elora found that hard to believe. Jarden wouldn't overlook someone on his trail for such a distance. He was too good of a forester for that.

The man seemed to sense her disbelief. He held up his hands placatingly. "Don't misunderstand. Your spy is incredibly good at what he does. I never would have been able to go undetected for any length of time if it weren't for a certain special advantage I have."

"And what advantage would that be?"

"Unh uh," he said, shaking his head. "Some secrets shouldn't be revealed so early in a partnership. It robs a person of potential future excitement."

Elora's eyes narrowed even more, and a crinkle appeared between her brows. "Give me one good reason why I shouldn't call for the guards."

"I'll give you two. First, you're not supposed to be out here either. Are you?" he asked with a sly grin. Her lips pursed in irritation.

"And the second?"

"Like I said. I want to help."

"Why would you want to help? I can tell from your accent that you're not from Yeatton."

Adrian stepped forward, his eyes locked onto hers. "No, I'm from Penningdon. But my sister was also cursed by the elf mage. She's been asleep for years, and I've spent every moment since trying to find a way to break the curse."

Elora felt a pang of sorrow at Adrian's words, and for a moment, her hopelessness resurfaced. "I'm sorry for your sister. But if you've been searching for years, why do you think you would be able to help me now?"

Adrian's eyes burned with determination. "Because I have important connections. What I don't have is soldiers. You have soldiers but not my connections. If we work together, we might have a chance at taking down the elf mage once and for all."

Elora studied him for a moment, considering his offer. She knew it would be risky trying to capture the mage. Her intel only provided dates and general locations. She needed much more information. How many elves would be traveling with him? What were their abilities? Would they have guards?" She studied the man carefully. The crickets chirped in the bushes nearby, and the moonlight gave the garden an ethereal glow.

"What kind of contacts do you have?"

"Elves," he said.

"From Allanar?"

"No," he admitted reluctantly. "From Elanora. They stayed out of the elven-goblin war, so they're much friendlier toward humans. I've met a few who disapprove of our mage friend and how he throws curses around as if they were rose petals." Adrian stepped closer and put his hands on Elora's shoulders, staring deep into her eyes. "They are elves. They can come and go in Allanar without raising any suspicions. They can find out anything we need to know. They can help us get the curse removed."

Elora felt a tingle run down her arms at his touch. Could she trust this stranger? She stared into his handsome face. Was he telling the truth? Was that a dimple in his cheek? Did she really find him attractive? Could it be...?

Focus, Elora, she thought. If Adrian was also fighting for the same cause, it might give her the edge she needed. Elora gently patted one of his hands and backed away from him. His arms dropped to his sides, and she was surprised that she missed the contact.

"Very well," she said. "But we must be cautious. We can't afford to make any mistakes. The elf mage is powerful, and he has many friends. We'll need to plan this carefully."

"Of course."

Elora gave him a small smile. "Good. Do you know where the barracks are?"

He nodded.

"Meet with Jarden tomorrow morning. I'll send him a message, and he'll be waiting for you at the entrance. He'll give you more information about the plan and our soldiers, and you can tell him what you know."

Adrian nodded and bowed before disappearing back into the bushes. Elora watched him go, feeling a strange mix of excitement and apprehension. She had never personally worked with anyone who wasn't from Yeatton before, let alone a stranger. But if it meant stopping the threat that had plagued her family for so long, it was a risk she was willing to take.

As she climbed back up the trellis and into her bedroom, she couldn't help but wonder if this might be it. Could she be close to breaking her curse?

Elora again sat before her mirror, and once again, her emotions threatened to etch a salty trail down her cheek. Just as they had the night before, but she couldn't allow them to escape now. Her maid, Rolena, stood behind her, fixing her hair for yet another outing with yet another eligible suitor. Roe worried about her princess enough as it was. Elora had to stay strong for her sake.

She had to stay strong for everyone. If she broke down, Roe, Deanna, her mother, her father, they would all break down with her. The weight of it was crushing her.

She tried to focus on the constant chatter Roe kept up as she arranged and pinned her hair. Roe was a good friend but not usually such a chatterbox. Elora wasn't fooled. Her maid had noticed her mood and was attempting to cheer her up. Well, she would let her. She could give way to her despair later when she was alone. If she could hold out that long.

"And they say the waterfall at the meadow is beautiful. With the rain we had the other day, it's going strong. You better not sit too close, or the mist might frizz your hair."

Elora forced out a chuckle, making it as light-hearted as she could.

"Maybe I shouldn't," she said with a grin, getting into the spirit of the conversation. "If the duke can't love me with frizzy hair, can he really love me at all?"

Roe stabbed her a little too hard with a hairpin.

"Ow," she protested, raising her hand to her head.

"He can love you with frizzy hair after you get married. For now, you need to show him your best side."

Elora frowned. "How about after one month? If we last that long. Can I show him frizzy hair after a month?"

Roe tapped a hairpin against her lips as she thought. "A month might be long enough."

"Long enough for what?" Elora asked with a laugh.

"For him to be so enamored with your beauty that he doesn't notice the frizzy hair."

"Ah. So, what's he like?" Elora examined her fingernails nonchalantly.

"You know I can't tell you that! Queen Callista has made it very clear that you need to meet these men without any preconceived notions." She wagged her finger at the princess through the mirror. "Gossip only serves to make us think the worst about people. It's rare that gossip relates any positive qualities, and even rarer that it relates any truth."

"Yes, of course. You're quite right." Elora nodded seriously. "So. Now that we've gotten the necessary protests out of the way, what have you heard?"

"Well." Roe bent down a little closer and lowered her voice as if someone were listening. "Becky, who works in the kitchen, ran into Martha at the market yesterday. Martha is Duke Ravendell's undercook. She said that he's very excited about finally meeting you. He thinks it's fate that he's one of the last Yeatton nobles to do so."

"Hasn't he been gone for the last five years on a diplomatic mission?"

Rolena nodded.

Elora snorted. "That's not fate. That's just life. He sounds a little dramatic."

"I agree. But Martha said he seemed convinced that he would be the one to win your love. He's even bringing his mother's ring to the picnic in case the situation seems ripe for a proposal."

Elora gasped and turned to face her friend. "A proposal! This is the first time I'm meeting him."

Roe just shrugged and turned the princess back around so she could finish arranging her hair.

"Maybe Mother was right," Elora said. "It might have been better if I hadn't heard this. I'm afraid that I'm beginning to dislike him already."

"Just give him a chance," Roe said, regretting her words. "Martha spoke of him with more humor than malice. If the servants like him, he can't be all bad."

"Perhaps, just a bit dramatic and immature?"

Roe laughed. "You could live with that, couldn't you?"

Elora groaned. "I don't know if I could."

"Well, whatever happens," Roe said, giving Elora's hair a final pat, "you'll look lovely while it does."

Kingdoms of Beauty Series

www.ingramcontent.com/pod-product-compliance
Lightning Source LLC
Chambersburg PA
CBHW021233250626
47155CB00008B/2998